NORMAL PEOPLE DON'T LIVE LIKE THIS

for Betty —
With so much pleasure!

NORMAL PEOPLE DON'T LIVE LIKE THIS

Dylan Landis

and all my best —

dylan landis

A Karen & Michael Braziller Book

PERSEA BOOKS/NEW YORK

Copyright © 2009 by Dylan Landis

The author wishes to thank the editors of the magazines and periodicals in which many of the stories in this book first appeared, sometimes in earlier versions: *Bomb*: "Hate"; *Colorado Review*: "Delacroix"; *Night Train*: "Fire"; *Quarterly West*: "Underwater"; *St. Petersburg Review*: "Excelsior"; *Santa Monica Review*: "Rose"; *Swink*: "Breakage"; and *Tin House*: "Jazz" and "Rana Fegrina".

In addition, "Breakage" appeared in *Gravity Dancers: Even More Fiction by Washington Area Women* (Paycock Press, 2009); "Jazz" appeared in *The 2004 Robert Olen Butler Prize Stories* (Del Sol Press, 2005) and *Do Me: Tales of Sex & Love from Tin House* (Tin House Books, 2007); "Rana Fegrina" appeared in *Bestial Noise: The Tin House Fiction Reader* (Tin House Books/Bloomsbury, 2003) and *The Best American Nonrequired Reading* (Houghton Mifflin Company, 2003); and "Rose" appeared in *Women on the Edge: Writing from Los Angeles* (The Toby Press, 2005).

Persea Books, Inc.
853 Broadway
New York, NY 10003

Library of Congress Cataloging-in-Publication
Landis, Dylan, 1956–
Normal people don't live like this / Dylan Landis.
        p. cm.
"A Karen & Michael Braziller book."
ISBN 978-0-89255-354-9 (trade pbk. : alk. paper)
1. Teenage girls—Fiction. 2. Nineteen seventies—Fiction. 3. New York (N.Y.)—Fiction. I. Title.

PS3612.A5482N67 2009
813'.6—dc22

                    2009009599

Designed by Rita Lascaro
Printed in the United States of America
First Edition

To Ari and Dean

Contents

NORMAL PEOPLE DON'T LIVE LIKE THIS

Jazz

It is not true that if a girl squeezes her legs together she cannot be raped.

Not that Rainey is being raped. She doubts it, though she is not sure. Either way, it is true that the thirty-nine-year-old male knee, blind and hardheaded, has it all over the thirteen-year-old female thigh, however toned that thigh by God and dodgeball. You may as well shove Bethesda Fountain into the lake as try to dislodge the male knee.

That's where she is: on her back, on the grass near Bethesda Fountain in Central Park. Angels darken in the dusk on the fountain's dry tiers, and Rainey watches through the slats of a bench. She had started to walk the lip of the muted fountain, but Richard wanted to inspect the thin silty edge of the lake.

Not far, he said. A constitutional.

How far is far, that's what Rainey wanted to know. She didn't care what a constitutional was.

The lake edge quivered and Rainey saw that the water was breathing. Richard dipped his hand in Rainey's hair and said, "You could turn the fountain on."

Richard plays French horn, and Rainey's dad says all horn players are a little strange. Rainey likes to court this strangeness because Richard is three-quarters safe, he is appreciative in ways that do not register on the social meter, he responds invisibly, immeasurably. She has tasted the scotch in Richard's glass. Her dad's attention was elsewhere. He was riffing on the piano in their living room, spine straight and hands prancing, head shaking *no no no it's too good*, the man up to his shoulders in sound. Her first taste had burned and she looked at Richard *why don't you just drink bleach* and he smiled *try growing up first*, and she was good at this kind of talking, eye dialogue, with nuances from the angle of the head. Then she swallowed without wincing and looked at Richard for affirmation and he raised his eyebrows *are you sure you want to go farther* and she arched her neck so his gaze would have something to slide down *I want to go far*, and she drank the entire rest of his glass.

At the lake near Bethesda Fountain, Richard extended two fingers with broad white moons under the nails. He tilted her chin so she stared at his big face against the bruised sky. "You generate energy," he said. "You could turn on a city of fountains."

The eighth-grade boys do not have pores.

Richard said, "You radiate power and light," and he led her, electric, to the grass.

Rainey has tea-rose oil between her toes, because one day a man might smell it there and be driven genuinely out of his mind, and she has a wedding band on her left forefinger because her ring finger is too small. Both of these things, the rose oil and the ring, she claimed from the medicine cabinet after her mother got into the cab. She looked for the plastic compact with its squashy white dome, but that was gone.

It is true that Rainey radiates power and light. And it is true that she loves making Richard say these things. She loves that he is a grownup and yet he seems to have no choice. This fascinates her, just as it fascinates her that mothers look at her strangely. They are like mirrors, these mothers, the way they register the heat disturbances that emanate from under her skin.

It could be true, but it could also be a lie, that a teenage boy can get an erection just by brushing against a woman's arm on the bus. Mr. Martin in sex ed was very specific about the circumstances: boy, woman, arm, bus. As Rainey interprets this it is the Broadway bus, an old green 104 lumbering uptown at rush hour, and the woman is eighteen, no, she is twenty-one, and carrying a white shopping bag with violets on it, and wearing a lavender cardigan. The top three buttons are open, no, the top four, but it is her slender, sweatered arm as she squeezes toward the back of the bus that engenders the event.

It is a lie that if a girl doesn't do something about the erection, it will hurt so badly that some injury will be caused. Mr. Martin said this too.

Rainey ran the tip of her tongue along the rim of Richard's glass and said, "When I'm sixteen, will you date me?"

"Only with your father's permission," Richard said. She waited for him to glance toward the piano, but he didn't.

It is a lie that Rainey will be allowed to live with her mother in Boulder when she is sixteen, because her mother belongs to an ashram now, and Rainey understands that by belongs to, her mother means belongs to, the way lipstick or leotards belong to a person. It is also a lie that her father and Janet are just friends. Rainey has plastered herself to the wall outside Howard's bedroom and listened to the strange symphony of sex—the oboe of a groan, the violin singing Oh my God, the cello that is her father murmuring into some part of the body that is bent or curved.

"I take it back," Richard said. "When you're sixteen I'll marry you."

Rainey is under Richard on the grass now and she gasps from his weight, and it is true that it sounds like desire, and it is true that she likes hearing herself make the sound.

Richard's hands are mashing her wrists. His hands have hair on the back. Andy Sakellarios, who might or might not be her boyfriend, has smooth hands. Richard is a fire she has lit, and men are flammable, and Rainey believes it is her born talent, the one she sees reflected in the mothers' eyes, to set the kind of flickering orange fire that licks along the ground. Rainey accepts the pressure of Richard's knee and hands like she might accept the force of a river before she lies down on its current. Outside Boulder the river had been colder than cracked ice on her back teeth. Rainey had let the water swirl her hair, let the cold polish her bones. She loved how surrender felt like a flower opening and she loved having the power to choose it. She ended up nearly a half-mile downstream where her mother found her at a campsite with boys, bikini dripping, drinking Miller from a can.

It was a lie that she had just taken one sip.

The soft grunts that squeeze from inside her are hers, but not hers. They are a lie and they are not a lie. Her toes smell delirious but Richard is crushing her lungs. Her lungs look like the fetal pigs in jars in the science room, and maybe gray like them too, because she loves to smoke. Smoking is one of the best things that ever happened to her.

"Give me that," her mother had said, and snapped the Miller can away from her.

The man with his knee between her legs and the heels of his palms bearing into her wrists says, "Jesus God, Rainey." He says, "I want to eat your hair."

It is a lie that he actually eats her hair, but it is true that he chews on it for a while. Her hair sounds crunchy between his teeth, like sand. She does not mind him chewing on it. She thinks how this is one more interesting thing a man can be reduced to. She wonders if sex is like math, like if you make a man want to eat your hair or go too far, does it follow that you balance the equation by letting him. And she exhales a sharp sigh whenever Richard moves, and it sounds like yes, when what she really means is let's go hear John Coltrane.

Rainey is on her back on the grass near Bethesda Fountain. There could be dogshit in the grass next to her, and Rainey wants Richard to roll off her so she can wrestle herself up, but then he might end up lying in dogshit, and this seems like terrible damage to inflict, especially on her father's best friend, who is supposed to be taking her to hear John Coltrane because her father had to play in the Village and couldn't go. John Coltrane plays three kinds of sax and he even plays jazz flute. She loves jazz flute, the way it rises hotly through the leaves of trees, then curls and rubs along the roots. Jazz flute lives about two stories off the ground. It is a reedy ache in a place she cannot name. How will Richard get her to Summerstage if there is dogshit on his back?

"Jesus," says Richard. "Somebody make me stop."

He releases one wrist and pushes her peasant blouse, with the scarlet and blue embroidery, up under her armpits. Rainey pounds on his back but her freed fist is soft as clay.

At school, where they are doing Oedipus Rex, Rainey has to hang herself from the climbing rope in the gym. She clutches the rope to her neck with both hands, and when she dies, Oedipus unfastens a pin from her toga. This always takes a few seconds too long because Oedipus, who is shorter, and chubby, trembles in the face of her power and light and her breasts being so incredibly present, like an electrified fence he has to fix without touching. And then he pokes his eyes out with the pin. It is just like that Doors song where the killer puts his boots on and then he pays a visit to his mother's room, and then Jim Morrison's throat releases this unholy cry.

Through the ground, Rainey feels the crowd gathering, she feels blankets unfolding on grass, she feels tuna-fish sandwiches nestling in wrinkled tin foil. She feels John Coltrane place his fingers on the soprano sax like it is her own spine. She feels how a concert swells before it starts and she wants to be there, she wants to lie on a blanket while Richard smells her toes and is driven insane, and she wants to feel the exact moment when the sound of the sax shimmies over the Transverse and toward the sky, changing the course of the East River and starting every fountain in the city.

At the campsite her mother had said: "This is what I flew you here for? This is what your life is about?"

It is probably true that all men want to go all the way, all the time.

It is true that when Rainey has her French notebook open she is designing the maxi-coat of her dreams, and bridal gowns including bridal miniskirts with trains and go-go boots, using agonizingly neat strokes with a pale pink Magic Marker. She makes the bridal gowns shell-pink because there is no white. Is this what her life is about? It is true that she plays a halting classical flute, and it is true that she lies and says she plays jazz. She is good at drawing clothes and being Jocasta. She is good at having a disturbing and emanating body.

Richard is eating her ear now. He does it like kissing. She turns her head away but that presents the ear more centrally. She wonders when he will want to get up.

She tries to talk but all she gets out is the word "what." She wants to say, "What time is it," so Richard will leap up, wiping grass off his knees, and say, "Oh, shit, let's go." But darkness has spilled into Central Park and if she talks too loud, gangs of boys might rustle toward them carrying moonlight on their knives.

In Boulder the boys at the campsite had been older. She told them she was fifteen and a half, that she played jazz flute and was dying for a smoke.

The boys smirked at the ground when her mother showed up. "Howard warned me to keep an eye on you," her mother said. She took an angry sip from the Miller can. Then she looked across the ring of stones where the fire belonged and said, "Thank you, gentlemen, for giving my daughter a beer. Did she happen to mention she's only twelve?"

"Not for long," Rainey said.

One of the boys had opened his mouth into the shape of a shocked twelve, and the blond boy with the gold earring and the cross had looked straight at the mother and said: Sorry, we didn't know. The cross made Rainey want to find the badness in this boy. She wanted to ignite him with a brush of her arm. She wanted to steal this boy from God.

"You didn't know," said her mother. She crumpled the can and tossed it into the ring of stones, splashing beer on the red dirt. Rainey's mother had that ripe thing going on. Her legs were tennis-hard from another life. The boy's eyes had flickered, or maybe it was his mouth, and Rainey looked over in time to see her mother half-smile, sardonic and quick. *Keep dreaming, Buster.*

Richard is licking near her armpit, which she shaved on Monday with Janet's razor. Today is Thursday. She has stubble but her toes smell like tea rose. Richard raises himself and licks along the underwire of her Warner's Miss Debutante bra.

"Richard," says Rainey, "get *off.*"

Richard says, "I'm not doing anything. I swear I won't do anything."

"You *are* doing something," says Rainey. He releases her wrists and she pushes on his shoulders. She wants to set fires and she wants to control how they burn. She likes going pretty far with Andy Sak, who is rendered both desperate and respectful by her power and light.

"I want to go to the concert," says Rainey. "Would you get *off?*"

She has known Richard since she was a toddler. She doesn't have to be polite.

"Five minutes," says Richard. He has freed a breast with his teeth. Rainey, propped on her elbows, sees how her breast lights up in the dark. It pumps out its resplendence like the sun. When Richard sucks on the nipple, the water roils up through the pipes in Bethesda Fountain and rains on the heads of the angels.

Rainey punches him on the head.

"Five minutes," he says. "In five minutes you'll be thirty-nine and I'll be fourteen and then we can go."

Rainey says, "Goddammit, Richard," and she is half-crying. She is not getting raped but he won't get up. She still wants to go too far but she is not sure how far is far.

"You think I just want that one thing," says Richard. "You think there's only one part of you that's special." He kisses her mouth again, and she lets him, even though he has a beard and his mouth does not have that boy-sweetness; it tastes of tobacco and steak.

"Thirteen," Rainey says, but there is clay in her mouth. Richard runs his tongue over her bare stomach. "I want to inhale you," he says. "I want to absorb you through my skin."

The current had been so strong. When she lay down on the river it held her up and swirled her like a big liquid hand, and she lay on it, releasing energy to the sky, letting the river be the stronger thing.

"You taste like music," Richard says. "You taste like jazz."

It might be true or it might be a lie that there is only one part of her that is special.

"Jesus God," says Richard. His tongue is in her navel and she has stopped punching his head because she is thinking, she is in the hand of the burning river, she is rising hotly through the leaves, and she hears him make the long sliding moan of the trombone.

Fire

Her mother cradled a teacup as if holding a dove. Toast cooled before her. If Leah thought hard across the table, she might arrange their confluence—fingers, toast. Toast, throat. Throat, esophagus, stomach, bowel. Leah had assembled the Visible Woman. She knew the route.

Her spoon ticked three times against the side of her egg cup.

"Please," her mother said. "If you could eat breakfast without tapping. Just this once."

Her father stared back and forth between them, looking newly amazed every morning. *His* breakfast never gave him any trouble: he dipped sausage links right into his boiled egg. "Sweetheart, let her tap. At least she eats."

"Mom eats," said Leah. "She just pukes it up after."

"And don't say puke." Her father slapped the table, then sank back. "What was wrong with upchuck? Upchuck was a perfectly good word."

"That one time," her mother said. "That was a stomach flu."

Leah waited for her father to say Oh horseshit, but he didn't. He kept pretending to read *The New York Times*, and Helen kept pretending to eat breakfast. Helen's eyes were shimmery and dark as her coffee, now that she'd stopped using milk. Her arms were slender as scissors. She sliced the toast into triangles, raised one halfway to her mouth. Hesitated. Looked at Leah. "Did you finish your homework?"

"You asked me last night," said Leah.

"This is true," said Helen. She put the triangle down, and performed some long, complicated surgery on the crust with the butter knife. Leah watched, fascinated. Her mother was a food magician in reverse. She performed fluid movements and distracting patter, and the food stayed right where it was. Her father glanced around the newspaper. Helen must have felt the glance land, because this time she got the toast to her bottom lip before pausing to check her watch.

"Darling, won't you be late?" she said.

Newspaper pages flapped, sparking the air with current events. *Hanoi* flashed by. *Mississippi* sailed over her father's shoulder. The pages settled into folds.

"Oh, I have a few minutes," said Leah's father, which meant *I can't leave till I see you chew*. But his chemistry class was at nine, and the subway to Queens, as he liked to say, was nasty, brutish and long.

"I don't suppose anyone cares that I loathe school," said Leah. She tried eating egg with her mouth open to see if anyone noticed.

"Progressive Day is a perfectly good school," said her mother. "Look at the lovely time Oleander has at Eleanor Roosevelt."

It was true, Oly got beat up a lot. In seventh grade she got her hair set on fire and a cigarette put out on her arm, and in September an eighth-grade boy, a boy who everyone knew was fifteen, pulled a knife on her. Oly ran. She said Leah wouldn't believe what he wanted her to do. She said Leah with her red hair, she'd get it worse. Roosevelt was where Leah was zoned for junior high before her parents sent her private.

She stared into the thin skull of her medium-boiled egg.

"Rainey Royal teases me every absolute day," she said.

"Rainey Royal," said her mother, "has problems you could not possibly understand."

Her father said, "Is she the one with the prodigious—"

"Leo," said Helen. "Please."

"She hates me. Her and Chris."

"She and Chris. *There's* a problem home. I believe that girl has to live with her grandmother."

Leah watched her mother spread a shine of jam on the toast, then scrape off the excess jam molecules. Her father looked relieved and started to rise. It took just one realistic food detail to unlock him from his chair. He kissed Helen's upturned forehead, messed Leah's hair before she could duck, then hesitated by the front door.

Helen bit off a piece of toast the size of a thumbnail and waved him off.

When he was gone, she pushed her plate away.

Lunch. Chris slid in on her right, Rainey on her left. They boxed in her damp orange tray with their own, like parked cars.

"You saved us a seat," said Rainey. She looked at Leah with delight.

"Why, Leah," said Chris. She sounded like Helen on the rare occasions there was fancy company at their apartment. "How *are* you?"

Leah concentrated on her plastic plate. Today was Greek salad. She nudged the olives over the rim. Plump and brown, they huddled on the tray like waterbugs.

"Yes," said Rainey, "how are you?" She attended closely to Leah's silence. "You are? Horny? Really? For Andy Sakellarios?"

Her voice rose, singsong. Even with head down and eyes closed, Leah could see her face. Rainey's hair was the exact brown of baking chocolate, thick and paper-straight. The bangs fell low over her eyebrows, and she had almondine eyes, like part Chinese. When she talked to boys, she locked her hands behind her neck so they could see her shaved underarms, watch her chest levitate. Leah studied Rainey only from the white part of her eye. One slice of a stare and Rainey would be on her case forever.

Rainey picked up one of the sidelined olives, inserted it between her lips and sucked. Leah could almost feel it—tongue spiraling the olive, a bitter taste blanketing the roof of the mouth. In her peripheral vision she saw Rainey's fingers meet her lips in a kiss of extraction.

"Delicious," Rainey declared, and dropped the pit, wet with saliva, onto Leah's lap.

She was afraid to move it.

She was afraid to move.

Across the table, Julie O'Dell mashed the wax paper from a homemade sandwich into a ball and sent it skittering, as if there were no such thing as death in this world, toward Rainey. "Cut it out," she said.

"You try it," said Chris. "She *likes* it. See?" She pocketed an olive in one cheek, displayed it between her teeth, chewed. Put her palm to her mouth. Then opened her fist over Leah's plaid skirt.

Nobody wore plaid skirts.

Leah looked at the two pits, more like scarabs now than waterbugs. She shook her skirt so they rolled onto the floor. Tapped surreptitiously on the bench—three left, three right—and ate a cube of feta cheese.

She hated feta cheese.

"Oh, Andy," sang Rainey. "Where are you, Andy? Leah has something to say to you."

Two tables over, Andy Sakellarios looked up. His gaze skated right off Leah's. When he met Rainey's eyes, he blushed.

"Listen," said Helen, while Leah spooned the skin off a chocolate pudding. She said: "I know I've raised this before, about not talking to strangers." It was a frequent drill. "Do you know why?"

Leah had already met a stranger. He walked up to her

and Oly in the park, where it was isolated, another Helen word, and asked to take their picture. He had a Kodak. He was polite. You perv, said Oly. The man apologized and went away. Leah didn't get it. Not the perv part, not the camera part. She only knew about Playboy pictures, and you had to look like Betty or Veronica for that.

"Yes, I know why," she said stiffly.

"Well, someone's daughter didn't know. It was in the paper. She followed a man up to his hotel room, and now she's dead."

Leah felt her face being studied, to see if this was having the proper impact. "Why?"

"He beat her to death," her mother said.

Leah stopped nibbling at the pudding skin. This was better than television, which they didn't have. "Why?" But what she also wanted to ask was: which hotel? There was a welfare hotel three blocks away, on 85th, where transistor radios plunged from the windowsills in summer. Once she saw a man in a wheelchair stab the air with a knife.

"The important question," said Helen, "is, why did she go? Leah, what if a strange man promises you money? What if he says he has a message from me? I'm just trying to make you cautious," she added. "I don't want to terrify you."

If Helen suspected she was terrified, the story would snap shut with the implacable finality of her tortoise-shell compact. Leah watched her mother weigh the benefits of going on.

"I'm always cautious," she said.

"Good," Helen said. "He used a hammer."

In Leah's imagination, the hammer flew through a number of possible aspects. Oly had never mentioned tools. Oly was learning stuff from her sister Pansy, who kept almost doing it. The bases, the positions, the four Fs—Leah relished the assembling of the facts of life, none of which she had the slightest intention of using. Ever.

"Why?"

Helen brooded into her teacup, then looked at Leah over its fragile edge. "He struck her twenty-seven times before she died," she said. "The police counted the marks. Do you know why I'm telling you this?"

She bled right into Leah sometimes. Inhabited her bones, inhaled her breath, spun stories behind her eyes. Leah watched this one unfold like she did the rest—because it was inescapable, because it was violent, because it was beautiful. The eyebrow cracking at the ridge like a broken cup. The hammer splitting knuckles as small and desirable as marbles. Purple flowers spreading under fingernails and skin. They looked like the bruises that mysteriously blossomed on Leah's thighs, the ones that made her father say, "Oh, my God, Leah, you have a quadriceps contusion."

She tapped the pudding bowl with noiseless fingers, three left, three right. Small movements.

"My mother never told me anything," Helen said, "but I believe in being honest. Are you listening, sweetie? A strange man tries to talk to you, promise me you'll run away."

Her mother said, "Another thing. If a man tries to touch you, never cry rape. No one wants to get involved. If a man bothers you, scream *fire*."

She said: "Is there anything you want to ask?"

"Why doesn't Chris live with her parents?"

"Leah, are you even listening?" her mother said. "This is your safety I'm talking about. This is your *life*."

Leah couldn't wait to tell Oleander about the hammered girl. Her mother must never read the paper, because she never warned Oly about anything.

Fluorescent light shuddered in the third-floor girls' room. Rainey posed against the radiator, and Chris pushed Leah toward her. She cranked Leah's wrist up behind her back. It hurt deep in the bone.

Rainey lit an Eve. It had flowers around the filter. She inhaled the French way, letting smoke curl from her lips and jet up her nostrils. Her nostrils were not much bigger than pearls. Leah had horse-nostrils; she hated her nostrils. Rainey ran the tip of her tongue across her teeth, lifted her chin, floated three practiced smoke rings toward the ceiling.

"I'm a baby," Rainey said at last.

Hypersexualized, Helen called her. Rainey's lips were slicked with Mary Quant gloss, which she dabbed on in class from a little black pot.

"Let me go," said Leah, twisting.

"*Let me go*." Chris, whining and jubilant, watching her own face in the mirror.

"I'm a sniveling baby," said Rainey.

"Okay," said Leah. "You're a sniveling baby." But she said it to the floor.

"Oo-ooh," sang Chris.

It was so humiliating, how she winced even before

Rainey slapped her. She felt her snot liquify, her hair tangle.

"I'm a sniveling baby with a big fat crush," said Rainey, fiercer. Her eyes burned with dark amusement. Chris yanked on Leah's arm. It felt like it might snap its hinge.

"I'm a sniveling baby with a big fat crush on Andy Sakellarios," said Rainey.

"Say it or say uncle," said Chris.

Oleander had a shiny crater near her hand where a girl put out a cigarette. The girl bummed the cigarette from Oly first. Then she asked for a light—right in the school stairwell, which should have told Oly that this girl wasn't afraid of anything—took one deep drag, looked Oleander in the eye, and jabbed the cigarette into her wrist. When Leah asked if she reported the girl, Oly looked at her with wild eyes. "I don't want the bitches to *kill* me," she said. "I just want them to leave me alone."

Leah whispered: "Uncle."

Her arm got released. Rainey and Chris locked eyes in the mirror. Their look made a bridge; she could walk across it. It was steely with malice, laced with plans.

"Why do you think they choose you as a target?"

The principal glanced at her mother as he said this, trying to establish that the grownups were on the same side. But her mother was not on anyone's side. She did not appreciate the summons.

"I know these girls, Mrs. Levinson," said Mr. Fitch. He tapped a pencil against his palm. The tapping had no pattern; he didn't realize that numbers mattered. "They're lively girls, but they don't mean any real harm. Perhaps Leah should consider what she brings to the situation."

Helen wove her fingers through her tumbling hair. Then she leaned forward in the blue plastic chair. Her voice was like the sheen on a lake. She would not want to hear about Leah kneeling in the girls' room, about the chalky taste of Pepto Bismol, about the cracked brown vinyl on the nurse's daybed where a roach once trickled out of the stuffing.

"All she has to do is ignore them, Mr. Fitch," her mother said, "and all you have to do is keep them apart. It doesn't seem that hard to me."

Mr. Fitch said, "Point taken," and nodded. "I'll do what I can. Leah's nearly a year younger—it may exacerbate things." He dipped the pencil between his hairless fingers, like a tracing. "Still, I do think she needs to ask herself: 'Why am I the only one they pick on?'"

It wasn't true. Sometimes they made Noah Lovell call himself a little faggot. Sometimes when they hedged him in, Noah Lovell looked wildly around the recess yard until he saw her, like spotting his reflection in a distant mirror. Once he gave Leah a ring with a plastic diamond. She threw it away. Rainey would pinch him, knowing he could never hit a girl, could never hit someone as pretty as her. Cut it out, Noah yelled, but the girls were relentless—"Say it," said Chris, "I'm a little faggot"—and always Leah turned away, because Rainey and Chris could switch from one target to the next with the silvery ease of minnows.

And yet she'd have stolen for Rainey, procured her cigarettes. She would let Rainey move her and shape her and demand absurd services that she would willingly grant, much like Barbie did to Midge in the privacy of her bedroom.

Her father brought home a pink diary that locked, and a fountain pen with cartridges. The ink was murky in the plastic tubes but shining and sweet when it flowed, unfurling thin ribbons of royal blue. Where it said "My Name," she wrote Leah Levinson. Where it said "My School," she wrote Progressive Day. Where it said "My Best Friend," she touched the nib to the paper, then lifted it, leaving a dark bead of hesitation that would never erase.

"Helen says you're having difficulties with a couple of the girls," her father said, while she blew on the wet script.

Leah didn't answer that one either.

"She says you feel they're mean." Her father settled on the corduroy edge of her bed and clasped his hands around a stork-like knee.

"They are."

"Is it real meanness? I'm sure it feels that way, but could it just be friendly teasing?"

His tone was gentle, a flag in a light breeze. Her father loved her; he wanted everything to be right.

She shrugged. "I guess."

Best subject: Math.

Worst subject: Lunch.

"That's my girl." His gaze ranged across her shelves, her desk.

"But it's mean teasing," said Leah.

The diary pages were edged in gold, and when she turned the key, she felt the pulse of the tumbling lock. "Where did you get this?" she asked. "It's gorgeous."

Her father reached out and smoothed a coil of hair behind her ear. It sprang back out. "You know, Leah, the thing to do with teasing, the only thing, is ignore it."

"Ignoring doesn't work." She drew tiny stars around the Leah Levinson, stars of David, not because she was Jewish, which she was, but because they were easier than the pretty five-pointed ones. The last time she tried ignoring, Rainey threw her gym shorts up the lockers where they bedded in a fur of dust.

"It helps to be consistent," her father said. "Next time they tease, pretend you're made of stone. An enchanted princess, made of stone."

Leah knew what would happen.

"I got you the diary," said her father, "so you could write about it. Sometimes that helps."

The diary smelled papery and new; it felt as private as breathing. She decided to write a book in it about her horrible school. She decided to write how the nurse wouldn't let her curl up on the vinyl daybed anymore, how she said, "Leah, this office is not here to solve your social problems." She decided to give the diary a pretty name. Dear Larissa, she would write each day. Dear Tamara. Dear Saralisa Jane.

Best characteristic: Walking with her feet turned out so grownups asked if she took ballet.

Biggest flaw: 32AAA chest. If there were such a thing as a 32 *concave*, that would be her. Also, the way when she tried to part her lips all glistening like Rainey's, her front teeth hogged the space. Also that there was no glisten, because she was not allowed to wear lip gloss. Also knowing what Noah Lovell knew, that in some mysterious, preordained, chemical manner, she had brought this on herself. Also that she was a sniveling baby with a big fat crush, though it was not on Andy Sakellarios.

In art Miss Giordano circled the worktables, pausing with occasional praise. When she got to Leah's seat she tilted her head and said, "If you could loosen up a little, Leah, your people wouldn't look so brittle, so stiff. Try sweeping curves, like this." She took the charcoal and made loose, breezy lines over the sketch. Leah could never permit that kind of ease. She would fall apart.

"Relax," said Miss Giordano. "Try doing it with your eyes closed, even."

When she moved on, Rainey said: "Yeah, Leah, *relax.*"

Everyone at their worktable looked up.

"Leah's gonna do it with her eyes closed," said Chris. "Pass it on."

Saturday. Helen pressed the pores of the receiver to her sweater and whispered, "It's that girl who hates you," but smiling, because obviously Leah had misjudged things.

Rainey said: "So you have to come to my house tomorrow or I'm grounded."

Then two layers of silence, as if her hand was over the phone.

"I can't," said Leah.

Her mother ran her finger along the spines of books in the shelves, pretending not to listen.

"Yes you can," said Rainey. "You have to. My dad had this meeting with Mr. Fitch. About you," she said darkly. "So you have to hang with me this weekend and let me be nice or I get grounded for like a *month*."

Leah listened to the double silence.

"I got the Jefferson Starship album," said Rainey. "Do you like them?"

Helen had moved into the kitchen with a flourish of privacy-giving. Leah could hear her listening. "They're great," said Leah. She waited for Rainey to say, Caught you, there's no such thing as a Jefferson—a Jefferson—but Rainey had moved on.

"We can do makeovers. I'm really good. I have all this makeup from when my mother left."

Leah's heart sprouted like a seed. It took such thin nourishment, like the lima beans she grew between wet paper towels for science. Maybe Rainey would be her new best friend. She'd confess what it meant: *when my mother left.* Did Helen know about this leaving? "Get that swivel out of your walk," Helen would say, all crisp, when Leah got home. "It's inappropriate."

Her father would say, "Aren't those jeans a little—help me out here, Helen—snug?"

Oleander would say, "She's a total bitch, why do you want to hang with her?" So forget Oly.

On the phone, Rainey said in her singsong voice: "I'll get ciggies."

Her mother said: "It's a sudden change in the weather, honey. I assume her parents will be there?"

Her father said: "I knew those girls would come around. Who wouldn't want to be friends with our Leah?"

Rainey lived in the top half of a brownstone. The front steps were pitted and jagged, and Leah couldn't tell if Rainey was rich for having half a brownstone or poor because it was falling apart. Leah lived in an apartment with one bedroom and no sunlight, but the doorman had gold braid on his uniform. She didn't know if that made her rich or poor, either.

Rainey opened the door and glanced past her, up the street. She wore a man's white shirt: collar up, a carelessness of open buttons, knotted at the waist. "Hey," she said.

Leah wondered what had happened to *hi*. "Hey," she said tentatively. It sounded okay. Plus she was wearing jeans finally, hiphuggers even, though they were still ink-dark and new.

"My dad won't be home for hours," said Rainey. Her hair smelled faintly of strawberry shampoo. Leah's was just Breck. "We can do anything we want."

"Oh," said Leah. "I thought your father—"

Rainey let the door slam. Leah thought crazily of mayonnaise jars, lids pierced with breathing holes, irrevocably screwed down.

She followed Rainey up three flights of metal-nosed stairs. Rainey's jeans were soft; they had faded to sky. How did she do that, make them fade? The hems had lapsed into worn, white fringe. Leah thought if she stared hard enough, the fringe might induce some kind of rapture, and then she realized it maybe had, because when she looked up again she was standing in a perfectly pink room. It might as well have been giftwrapped. Even the ceiling was pink.

"You can sit there," said Rainey, and pointed to a canopy bed. "I just have to finish."

Leah took her place gingerly on the edge of the bed. Rainey sat at a vanity, a real one, with a mirror and a skirt. Black plastic pots, like fat checkers, were scattered across the top. When Rainey searched among them they clicked against the glass.

"I'll do you next, okay?"

Rainey might stroke her eyelids. She might touch her lips.

"Okay," said Leah. She couldn't breathe. It was critical that she leave this house a different person. Maybe they could put on a record soon, Lulu, or the Doors. Leah had one album, *Hums of the Loving Spoonful*, because when her father took her to Sam Goody as a treat, she did not know what was good. Rainey had a whole stack of albums and her own phonograph. She had pink walls like petals, and pink fabric swooping over the bed. Leah's room was all white and navy blue, and books alphabetized on shelves.

"This is so pretty," she whispered. "It's like being inside a shell."

"My dad's girlfriend did it." Rainey appeared to be counting eyelashes in the mirror. "I wanted to paint it black, but my dad had a spasm."

"Where's your mom?" Leah asked this carefully, as if she were holding an expensive plate.

"Boulder," said Rainey. "I get to go live with her when I'm sixteen. She rides horses and everything. I've got all her clothes, too, the ones she didn't take."

Helen didn't own a vanity. She would not be going to Boulder anytime soon and leaving her clothes behind. Leah's heart flamed. She wanted her life to surge forward in a great glamorous rush.

Rainey lifted her chin, closed one eye and ran the tip of her pinky above the lashes. "Soft Camel," she said reverently, and held the eyeshadow out for Leah to admire. It was a whispery color, like the pale dust that clumped unbidden under her bed. And behind the talk Leah heard the texture of Rainey's voice: folds in a piece of silk.

"Do I look sixteen?" Rainey blinked at her. "Sometimes I go out with my dad and people think I'm his girlfriend. I'm more developed than she is, though. I think she's jealous. Once she bought me this flannel nightgown and I cut it into a micro-mini and she had a cow. *Wait*," she hissed, and lifted a finger, listening to the house.

Leah touched her housekey though her pocket..

"You're so lucky having green eyes," said Rainey, relaxing. "I wish mine were something exotic, like violet." And then she jumped up, jarring the vanity so the little pots clicked and slid, and ran out of the room.

As if she knew the doorbell would ring. "Don't move," she called from the hall.

Leah prayed: please God let it not be Chris, let it be her

father, please let me tap six sets of three with each hand before Rainey comes back. She tapped the spread. It was too soft; it was no good.

Base, she whispered, furiously anointing the bed. It wasn't Base. She heard giggling, whispers on the stairs, someone getting jostled.

Rainey spilled into the room, dropped crosslegged to the shag rug, made little bounces of excitement. She seemed to have forgotten about the makeover. Behind her, Chris planted a hand on each side of the doorway, leaning in. "Now we can have a party," said Rainey. "Sit," she told Leah, patting the rug.

Leah slid off the bed and sat.

In the doorway, Chris dangled her embroidered bag, and Rainey stopped its swinging and rifled it. She extracted a half-pack of Marlboros, cellophane gaping. The sharing of the purse was so intimate, so casual, Leah nearly stopped breathing again.

"Does your dad ever come upstairs?"

Chris and Rainey glanced at each other.

"Yeah," said Rainey. "He comes up. So what?" She lit two cigarettes, handed one up to Chris, and tossed Leah the pack. Then, just as Leah was feeling excluded, Rainey struck a match for her. Leah dipped her cigarette into Rainey's cupped hands, received the flame with eyes cast down.

Chris sent a long jet of smoke toward her face.

"Don't be scared," she said. "You're not scared, are you?"

They looked at Leah with interest.

"No," said Leah.

"Liar," said Rainey. She looked happy. Leah couldn't tell how Rainey wanted her to feel, or she would try to feel it.

"That's good you're not scared," said Chris. "Cause we're gonna get high."

Leah knew about getting high, because once she watched Oleander do it: take a can of Reddi-Whip off the dairy shelf at Sloan's, press the red plastic tab and suck in the hissing gas. Oleander laughed until she looked like someone else. Leah hated that, when people changed. She put the can back on the shelf. Oly just kept laughing.

"High on what?"

"Howard's pot," said Chris.

"Howard?"

"My dad," said Rainey.

Low in her stomach, where it was starting to hurt, Leah felt the word *uncle* forming.

"I can't," she said, and swirled a finger though the pink carpet.

"Higher than fucking kites," said Chris.

"I could wait downstairs," said Leah. "You know, while you do it."

Chris adjusted herself in the doorway, expanding slightly. Leah remembered the double silence, a hand over the phone.

"You might get grounded," said Leah, in case Rainey forgot.

"Howard wouldn't ground her if she burned down the house," said Chris.

"He'd ground me if I burned down his girlfriend's

house," said Rainey, and lifted her voice to a trill. "Oh, Howard. Oh, Howard. Oh . . . oh . . . "

They cracked up.

"I ought to go," said Leah.

She might as well try to duck under a wall, the way Chris didn't move.

"Oh, come *on*," said Rainey, getting to her feet. She clasped Leah's arm and pulled her as if she wanted to shake her, or embrace. Leah went stiff and lost a few degrees of balance, and her upper arm touched Rainey's breast. Some part of her altered, ripened, with that involuntary pressure. The breast, the left one, had more presence than Leah would have guessed. It felt like the calf of a leg, and like something more.

"Come on," Rainey said. She could have been pleading. "You can't leave now. We're going up on the roof."

Leah had never been on a roof. People fell from roofs; pigeons sailed from the parapets where people fell.

Still, she let Rainey prod her to the base of the narrow stairs. They all looked up. It was the last flight, dead-ending at a metal door. Above the door a skylight bulged like an eye. The steps looked slippery with sun.

"I don't know why I'm here," said Leah.

And then Rainey said something she would never forget. "My dad told me if you're scared of something, do it."

She, who was born knowing rules. She knew the rule about tapping in threes, the one about stacking coins. She knew the rule that if a looseleaf hole tore, she must rewrite the page. She knew the rule about touching all four corners of the switchplate when she stood dripping in the tub; this protected her from wanting to flip the switch, just to see.

But never did she know there was a rule for fear.

She put a foot on the stairs, taking a slow, sweaty inventory of her pocket as she climbed: housekey, token, folded five-dollar bill. The five dollars was mad money. Crazy money, she used to think, until her mother said no, it's in case you get mad at the person you're with and need to take a cab.

On the seventh step, because Leah always counted, she realized that Rainey and Chris were still waiting below and had launched her, alone and stupid, to the roof.

She took the key out and prayed God to make it a lucky charm, to make it Base. Then she squeezed the key three times, turned around, and sat.

"We won't lock you out," said Rainey, looking up from the base of the stairs. "We just want to see if you trust us."

Leah was the stone princess. She let Rainey talk.

Rainey nudged Chris. "You go," she said.

Chris stopped hanging back from the banister and climbed up to where Leah sat and kicked her ankle, not fighting hard, just sneaker-hard. "We're *trying* to be *friends*," she said. "Come on, get up."

Everything about her was bigger than Leah: her pupils like drills, the shoulder-width of her.

"God, you're pathetic," said Chris, and clomped downstairs.

That's when Leah realized, in the pour of dirty sunlight,

that Chris parted her hair with fingers instead of a comb, and that her nose turned up a little, like a pig's. Through Helen's eyes she considered the swell of flesh above Chris's braided leather belt. She thought about these things, and in thinking them she ran a tender finger along the edge of her fear.

"You're the pathetic one, *Chris*," said Leah. "You're a pathetic *bitch*," she said. Actually, she was shouting. Screaming almost. Chris stared up at her with her mouth dropped open.

"You're *stupid*," said Leah in this new screaming voice she had never heard before, coming from some inside place she had never even visited. "You're so stupid your own parents don't want you."

It was just like her father said at Passover. God didn't part the Red Sea for the Jews till they showed they were ready to act. "You think He drained it like a tub?" her father said. "Hah! He said, 'Roll up your trousers, gentlemen. Step right in. Show some conviction.' And He didn't part a drop of water," her father said, "until our people had plunged in up to their necks."

Leah, neck-deep, waited briefly for God to reach through the skylight and pull her through. Then she waited for Chris to at least cry. Finally she understood that neither of these things were going to happen. The three of them, together, watched them not happen. Chris just looked up the stairs at her from someplace dark, as if she had fallen into a hole.

"You are so mean," said Rainey, and she started up the steps.

To Leah's astonishment, she did not seem to mean Chris.

They would never let her go. They would lock her out on the roof. This was as far ahead as she could think.

"Mean and dead," Rainey said, stepping up to her. "You are just so dead, missy."

Or they would push her downstairs. This stuff happened. Look at Oly.

Her fear had an edge and the edge was jagged, like the key in her palm. She squeezed it three times three, but she barely felt its ziggurat bite as it cut into her lifeline, or Rainey's face.

A wail, like twisting metal.

Rainey slipped. She fastened one hand to her face. When the key fell it sounded like a quarter dropping.

"My eye," said Rainey. She was frantic and crying, and Leah wanted to rescue her. "My eye, Chris, you have to look at my eye." But she wouldn't take her hand away, even when Chris pulled at her wrist.

"It was a joke." Chris was shouting, or whispering, Leah could not tell. "We never had any pot. It was a joke, to see if you had the guts."

A spray of damp, satiny hair was caught under Rainey's hand.

"You could've said no," said Chris, and her voice was a siren now. "You didn't have to do this."

But she was wrong. Everything happened exactly as it was going to happen.

There was noise all around her, in the hall at the top of the brownstone. Chris saying, "Where's Howard?" Begging:

"Think, Rainey, I can't call Howard if you don't tell me where he is," and Rainey saying, "No, no," as Chris tried to peel her hand away. And beneath that a third layer of sound, a whispered chant that had to be her.

One word, over and over. "Fire," she said, "fire, fire," unable to remember why, knowing even the roof would be better than this.

Rose

Leah's grandmother, Sophia Rose, washed and dried her dinner plates, stacked them in the oven and set it on broil. She hid her pearls in the toilet tank, where they coiled under a rubber flap and created a perpetual flush.

"Nine is green," said Grandma Rose. "Four is red. Mint tastes like flashes of light."

Leah's parents decided it was time. They said Leah could stay with any friend she wanted. Oleander, said Leah. Helen and Leo were so busy gabbing on the phone to the social worker in Pottsdam and the Hertz people on 77th Street and the grandmother's bank, they didn't say no.

"I don't see why you have to put her away," said Leah, watching Helen fold tissue paper into her clothes—a winter-white sweater, because fall came early upstate, and a herringbone silk scarf. Helen hated wind in her hair.

"Leah, this is painful for me," said Leo. He was tethered to the phone in the hall. "But it's better than letting her die in a fire. And she can't communicate her needs. Her mind is deteriorating."

Grandma Rose's mind looked like her bedroom, Leah decided. It was a wonderful room. Hair pins napped in the rumpled bed. Dark hairs from her wiglet drifted into the cold cream. Tubes of Bain du Soleil lost their caps and slid into open drawers, releasing the oily fragrance of summer into white nylon bloomers. Nor did Sophia Rose seem to register, when Leah was allowed to stay with her, that Leah smoked in the basement, riffled through her grandmother's pocketbook and skimmed every paperback with a passionate couple on its cover.

"Why do they mix up the colors?" Grandma Rose said, peering over Leah's shoulder at a title. "O isn't red." The word was "romance."

"Red like a heart?" said Leah.

"My shayna maideleh," her grandmother said gently. "O is as white as an onion."

"She'll burn down the house if she keeps baking the plates," said Leo, gently.

"Maybe that's how she wants to go," said Leah. "Maybe the flames will talk to her."

Her father took his palm off the receiver and said, "Do we need a lawyer for that?"

"I wish I heard colors," Leah said loudly. "I bet red sounds like a piano. I bet yellow sounds like Dusty Springfield." She tapped the suitcase, three left and three right. But her parents kept getting ready to drive off and kidnap her grandmother. Oleander, when Leah telephoned, said sure.

"Don't you have to ask your mom?"

"Ask what?" said Oly. "Just bring your stuff. You won't believe what's going on here."

The night roof was alive. It ticked and scraped. Tarpaper crackled where no one walked. Ventilation fans flashed in their cages.

"This is where we're gonna do it," said Pansy. She hugged a damp Sloan's grocery bag containing a towel, two joints, and a rubber stolen from her and Oly's father.

Ten stories below the night roof, the brakes of buses sang. Leah wondered if she could make herself jump off a parapet. Then she couldn't stop wondering. Fly or die, fly or die. It was like standing in the bathtub and wondering should she touch the switch. Some thoughts she couldn't control when they cycled through her brain. Mrs. Prideau, who was Pansy and Oly's mother, did not have this problem. When they left the apartment Mrs. Prideau was standing in the kitchen, spooning ice cream out of the Schraft's box and writing on some typed papers in red pencil and ignoring the most amazing things. She ignored the leak under the sink that was wetting the grocery bags. She ignored the paint hanging from the ceiling like notepaper. She ignored that Oly and Leah threw eggs from the windows sometimes, or that Mr. Prideau slept by himself in the second bedroom because it was cheaper than divorce.

"Going to howl at the moon?" she said. "Don't fall off." God, Leah loved Mrs. Prideau.

Standing pipes, tall as people, stuck straight up from the tar. Leah tried to act casual in the face of the enemy. She edged closer to Oleander. "I bet those pipes move when we're not looking," she said, knowing it sounded crazy. "I bet they're like the roof police." The pipes tried not to look alive. Meanwhile Leah was tapping like crazy, fingers jammed in her pockets so no one could see.

Oleander fixed it. She touched each pipe, calling PLP— public leaning post. *Fly or die*. Meanwhile, Pansy started up the metal ladder to the water tower, which stuck up high above the roof. This was worse than the roof police. The water tower had no windows. It had no mercy. Leah imagined climbing. Then she imagined spilling over the edge, grasping at walls all slimy below the waterline.

Fly or die, fly or die, she whispered. She prayed God would lift her out, and while she prayed she quit breathing. Pansy Prideau crammed the Sloan's bag between the ladder and the curving base of the tower.

She climbed down again, flipping her hair.

"No one's gonna notice *that*," Pansy said.

Leah, enraptured, remembered how Pansy slept on her stomach because she rolled her hair around Minute Maid cans. She remembered how Mrs. Prideau was downstairs letting ice cream melt in her mouth, and reading and maybe smoking at the same time, and that tomorrow night she and Oly would sneak back up and watch Pansy do it.

Pansy stood at a parapet and looked down at the singing buses. A plane blinked through the black sky toward her ear. It disappeared into her head, then eased out the other side, propelling through waves of her Minute Maid hair.

That's when Leah inhaled—worshiped the night roof, remembered to breathe.

Saturday morning the milk smelled bad, so they got to eat Trix from the box. Then they went stealing. Leah palmed a Chunky at Manny's Fountain on Broadway just to feel it nest in her hand, silvery and square. At Ahmed's Candy & Cigarette, Oleander slid a comic down the back of her jeans. Leah knew just how it felt, slippery and stiff. She wanted to read it but Oly trashed it down the block. "No one reads Archie anymore," said Oly. Leah kept her hands out of the garbage. She liked to admire Veronica's bust, but she knew enough not to say it.

Leah and Oly, they were magnetic. Sweet things clung to them. When they stole, they had secrets, and when they had secrets, they shone.

They ducked under the turnstiles on 86th and changed subways twice and did Lord & Taylor's, where they tried on five brassieres each. Leah put back four and Oleander put back three. Then back down the clacky wood escalators to the main floor, where Oly stole the White Shoulders eau de toilette tester without even smelling it, just vacuumed it into her purse.

"You ditz," said Leah. "My grandmother wears that." Then she browsed at Christian Dior, smiled at the lady and stole the Diorissimo tester. She didn't smell it first because she knew it from the heartbeat of her mother's wrist.

Leah's mother knew all about department stores. She dispensed strange and dangerous facts. She said department stores had lady guards who only pretended to shop. They lingered over gloves or garters, but were actually spies. "They watch your hands, and they look for women who glance around," Helen said. "At night they check the ladies' rooms, so no one sleeps over on those lovely *chaises longues*." Helen was eating again, twelve hundred calories a day, and she worked for a decorator, ordering fabrics and sketching drapes. At night she studied pictures of French chairs.

"Don't glance," Leah warned. Oly had stopped at wallets.

But Oly couldn't help it. What Leah did was, she listened with her skin. Leah's skin was electric and it knew when she was invisible, and that's when she made things disappear. Then she tapped on the counter or in her pockets or even on the floor, as if she'd dropped a safety pin. Three left, three right. It made her safe, plus it was something she had to do.

The girls burst out of the same glass slot in the Lord & Taylor's revolving door. They walked fast with their heads down, except Oly kept glancing back.

"Holy Mary mother of God pray for us sinners now and at the hour of our death Amen," she said. Her eyes were like penlights.

"When can I throw up?" said Leah. Because that's what stealing made her want to do, after.

"In the park," said Oleander fiercely. "Puke in the park."

In Central Park Leah threw up behind a bush and spit nine times, three times three, to clean her mouth. They bought Creamsicles and walked to Oly's apartment, except on the way they did the Grab Bag on Broadway, where the clothes were all burlap and ribbon and lace— artistic, Helen said. Under glass, silver earrings lay on black velvet and tarnished in their sleep. On the counter, beaded earrings dangled from a rack; you could strum them with a finger.

"Steal me," they whispered.

Things spoke to Leah often. She did what they said.

Saturday evening, no one said a word about dinner. Mrs. Prideau sat on her bed and turned her manuscript pages and watched Pansy get ready, as if this was what daughters were supposed to do, go out with boys. Sometimes all Mrs. Prideau said about dinner was "Oh, just forage," and Leah hoped she would say this soon so they could eat more Trix.

Pansy leaned over the bathroom sink, dabbed blue shadow on each eyelid and stared at herself in the mirror. Then she smiled, or snarled, so her teeth showed. Pansy had a face like a Madame Alexander doll, the expensive kind in glass cabinets at FAO Schwartz—round glass eyes in a creamy round face. Pansy looked like a cross between seven and seventeen. Leah watched her from the doorway, hoping to learn something. What she learned was how to put on blush. First you grin. Then you rub lipstick on the part of your cheek that sticks out like a cherry tomato.

Oleander opened bureau drawers and slammed them, pulling out tops and shoving them back in. No one at Oly's had private drawers or private shirts or even private beds, because Mrs. Prideau and Oly and Pansy shared two beds in the one big bedroom and didn't have space for private anything. Sometimes this made Leah so jealous she could die and sometimes it made her want to go home and straighten her desk. A bandanna halter came out with a froth of socks and Oly put it on and went in the bathroom and sprayed a cloud of Right Guard around her armpits.

"Oh, good, deodorize the toothbrushes," said Pansy, fanning at the cloud.

"Any toothbrush of yours it's automatic B.O.," said Oleander, and sat the can on the sink, where Leah knew it would mark the porcelain with a ring of rust.

"Any toothbrush of yours it's automatic pus," said Pansy.

"Oh, shit, here they go," said Mrs. Prideau, and looked at Leah like they might actually share some sliver of understanding. She lit a clean cigarette with the old one and jabbed the old one out. The butts in her ashtray were all kissed red at one end and bent jagged at the other.

"Your parents go anyplace fun?"

"Upstate," said Leah. "They're kidnapping my grandmother."

Mrs. Prideau's eyebrows lifted into question marks, thin and elegant. "Are they taking *her* anyplace fun?"

"Old folks' home," said Leah. "Her mind is deteriorating."

"Really." Mrs. Prideau looked at Leah like she was trying to figure out where to insert a key. "How can they tell?"

Leah shrugged, but Mrs. Prideau kept waiting, so she went on. "She sticks plates in the oven and they melt. She's going to burn down the house."

"She might," said Mrs. Prideau. "If she has dementia, your parents are probably doing the right thing."

In the bathroom Pansy said, "Gloss or frosted?" and Oleander nudged her out of the mirror so she could put blue eyeshadow on too.

"Plus," said Leah, "she sees things. She says nine is green, vowels are white, stuff like that."

She hated the way she sounded, as if Sophia Rose were someone else's crazy grandmother, so she started biting her cuticles.

Mrs. Prideau sat straight up and looked at Leah. She didn't say stop biting. "Well," she said, "I don't know about the vowels. A is light pink and E is almost scarlet. But nine is definitely green."

Mrs. Prideau was not beautiful like Helen. She had short spiky hair and she wore black turtlenecks and jeans. She had ink on her fingers instead of nail polish. But there was some kind of light that went on inside her, and at that moment Leah thought if she stood very still, the light might shine on something she needed to see.

"Not all vowels," Leah said carefully. "She said O and I were white like an onion. I thought it was because they're in the word onion."

"No, it's because they're white," said Mrs. Prideau. "I also see Q and X as white, but you don't run into that as often."

Leah didn't move. Tap now, her brain instructed, but for the first time in her life she disobeyed.

"It's called synesthesia," said Mrs. Prideau. "It runs in families, but it missed my daughters. You too?"

Leah shut her eyes and concentrated. She wanted Mrs. Prideau's voice to reveal a shape, a scent. She thought it might smell like Diorissimo, or float like a string of pearls.

"It missed me," she said.

Pansy walked out of the bathroom with frosted white lips. She looked perfect. Leah wanted to lay her down flat to see if her eyelids would glide shut. "Tell her what her name tastes like, Mom," she said. "Mine tastes like tea biscuits."

"Very thin biscuits," said Mrs. Prideau. "Leah tastes like cucumber."

"It could be worse," Pansy said. She spotted Leah's shoplifted earrings on the bureau, threaded one into her ear. "We had a babysitter once named Renee whose name tasted like pennies."

"*Syn*, together, *aisthesis*, perception," said Mrs. Prideau, not even flicking her eyes toward Pansy, who was taking one of her cigarettes. "It means the senses work in pairs. It's a gift. Synesthetes are often artists," she said. "Scriabin had it. Kandinsky, though he may have been faking. Nabokov. Is your grandmother creative?"

"No," said Leah, who had no idea what she was talking about.

"I bet she is," said Mrs. Prideau. "Kandinsky said synesthetes were like fine violins that vibrated in all their parts when the bow touched them."

The doorbuzzer made its jagged rasp. "Oh my God," said Pansy, "it's Robbie," and she left the cigarette burning on the bureau, a fringe of ash hanging over the edge. Oleander glanced at her mother, whose lap was spread with red-penciled pages, picked the cigarette up and brought it to her lips. Leah couldn't believe what she was seeing. Her parents would have a coronary.

"We are the bows from which our children as living arrows are sent forth,'" said Mrs. Prideau. She looked at her younger daughter with the cigarette and closed her eyes, as if she were searching for something deeply internal.

"Kahlil Gibran," she said, opening her eyes and, as Leah wondered if she would ever understand, "Don't be discouraged, Leah. We never know what we inherit."

They watched her.

They hid behind the elevator shed and watched her on the roof.

He did everything exactly in order, first base, second base, third base, home. Leah liked it, liked the way his hands traveled on Pansy and the way Pansy let her body be a highway for them. He pulled her jeans off. There wasn't any underwear. This was a revelation, that a person could not wear underwear. They saw his hands move where his fly was and then he pushed onto her and Pansy made a sound like she had stepped on a piece of glass, and he put his hand over her mouth. When he took it away he kissed her. Then he pushed some more. This got boring, but Oleander kept saying "Jesus" under her breath, so Leah just hung back a few minutes and didn't look, and thought about what it was that they might have inherited, her and Oleander and even Pansy, who was fifteen and barely spoke to them.

The boy peeled something off his penis and tossed it away like a piece of skin he had shed. He pulled up his jeans. He lit a joint and Pansy took it from him. The roof police didn't do a damn thing. They just stood there.

They were just pipes.

"Was that *home?*" said Leah.

"Yeah," said Oleander, "Jesus," and they were breathing words more than talking them. They carried their sandals so they wouldn't scuff and moved toward the stairwell cautiously, as if stepping over puddles.

"It hurts," said Leah, amazed.

"Only when you lose it," said Oleander, and Leah felt a rose open in her body, felt a release as its petals fell open and flew apart, and she wondered what she had lost, and why it did not hurt.

Rana Fegrina

Angeline Yost keeps a switchblade in her sock.

Angeline Yost has B.O.

Angeline Yost did it in her parents' bed and a week later they had crabs so bad they were in their *armpits*.

The Gospel of Angeline Yost is graven into desks with housekeys and the blood of Bics; it is written in the glances of girls—low arcs of knowing that span the hallways and ping off the metal lockers.

Angeline Yost walks with her books soldered to her chest.

Angeline Yost bites her nails until a quarter-moon of roseate nailbed rises at the top of each finger. When she laughs, her eyes narrow; the laugh is bitter and quick in her throat.

Angeline Yost once stuck a hot dog up inside herself and couldn't get it out and her parents had to drive her to the hospital.

Angeline Yost eats lunch with two older girls: Dierdre who has a forehead broad as a man's, and a girl whose brother Keith went to jail for almost killing a guy. Dierdre and the other girl are blond the way Angeline is blond, with ribbons of brown raveling along their side parts. They are juniors. They could get Keith to fuck you up. No one calls them a slut.

In the beginning is the word and there is no making it go away. Leah's finger polishes the dark scars in her honeyed desk: the jagged S, the glottal LUT. The word is appended to the initials A.Y. In Leah's mind the name ANGELINE is gleaming and round. It is the razor and the apple, both: lethal and sweet.

When she gets tired of reading her desk she tries reading Mr. Jabor's T-shirt backwards, searching for hidden meaning. Forwards it says I'D RATHER BE WRITING MY NOVEL in inky typewriter-type.

Mr. Jabor's hair stands straight up which is why he cuts it to a fuzz. His arms jut from his sleeves like splints and he has earnest knees, perpetually bent. Mr. Jabor is the only teacher Leah knows who comes to work in sneakers. She gets a good look at them because she sits in the second row, and Mr. Jabor reads poetry standing on his desk.

The kids are supposed to call him Rick.

"Walt is not just another dead poet, ladies and gentlemen," Rick says. A cigarette bobs and jabs in the corner of his mouth. The freshman English class stares at him much of the time, waiting for him to light up. Sometimes he does.

"Listen to this," says Rick. "This is so good it'll make you want to pee in your pants."

Leah considers the option. In three and a half periods she will have to carve something far more elemental than a word into the thoracic-abdominal cavity of *Rana Fegrina*, a creature as tender and green as a gingko leaf. Everyone will look at her because she got a bad lab partner, a partner who has been held back and has B.O., and this will somehow appear to be Leah's fault and she will have to mouth-breathe for the entire fifty-five minutes.

The atmosphere is not a perfume, says Rick, his knees shooting off little sparks with each bounce. *It has no taste of the distillation, it is odorless, it is for my mouth forever, I am in love with it.*

Rick's sneakers squeak on his desk and Leah looks away. She hates Rick's sneakers for being so excitable and sympathetic and she hates the name Walt.

Rick has been reading poetry to them all semester, Coleridge who was an opium addict and John Donne whose son died, and the one who peed in his pants over a Grecian urn, Keats. No matter what Rick says, Leah cannot name one thing that poetry heals. For example, poetry does not heal adenocarcinoma of the lung. Leah's father smells like formaldehyde and he's still alive, and that is a mystery not even Walt can explain.

She writes on the inside cover of her notebook: Rana Levinson. Leah Fegrina. Rana Leah Fegrina.

I will go to the bank by the wood and become undisguised and naked, says Rick. *I am mad for it to be in contact with me.*

Leah hears tittering. Peripheral movement of hands, a shard of briefly-floating white: a note is being passed. Leah does not have the kind of school friendships that involve communication by note, or even, for the most part, by speech. This is due partly to being a girl five-nine with acutely red hair, which causes people to look at her, which causes her to think that large bells are clanging above her head.

Rick grips his book with both hands, like a preacher. "This man is talking about rejoicing in the physical universe," he says. "Are you listening? Because some of you really need to hear this." *My respiration and inspiration, the beating of my heart, the passing of blood and air through my lungs.*

It is thirty seconds to 10:35. Even Rick can see that. The instant his shoulders deflate, backpacks slam onto desks; fingers fly over clasps.

"Wait!" yells Rick. "Gimme one thing you learned from Walt. One thing."

"Get naked in the woods," says Andy Sak.

Leah doesn't turn around because Andy Sakellarios is too lovely to look at directly, just as when Leah's father opens his eyes anymore in his metal bed and looks directly at his daughter, she has to study a crease in the sheet. The crease floats over his chest like the ghost of his scar. Leah knows that Andy Sak's mouth is slightly open, like a cup. She knows that the curvature of his skull is elegant in the way that mathematicians use the word.

"Yeah?" says Rick. "You're close. Relish the natural world, and remember that you are a part of it."

Kingdom Animalia. Subkingdom Metazoa. Section Deuterostomia. Phylum Chordata. Subphylum Vertebrata.

These are the places where Leah seeks beauty: in the classification of living things, in books arranged by height, in closets with hangers precisely one and one-half inches apart and clothing zoned by color. She seeks purity in the blamelessness of a clean-swept desk. She seeks forgiveness in each new sheet of loose-leaf paper. Class Amphibia. Order Anura. Biological name Rana Fegrina of the long green hands.

They've had three days to memorize the exact position of the frog in the biological universe. Leah was born with the words in her bones; she took ten minutes.

"Remember the fingerprick?" says Mr. Lack. "If you had trouble with the fingerprick, raise your hand."

The arms of girls shoot into the air. Leah's rises halfway. A few boys who had trouble with the fingerprick start shoving, or maybe it's the word that gets them going. Not finger. The other one. Angeline Yost doesn't raise her hand. She's ransacked the dissection kit without waiting for instructions and is stroking the scalpel down the inside of her arm, dragging it lightly, almost weightlessly, so no weal of red unrolls behind it.

Leah takes a small step back.

"Those of you with hands aloft," says Mr. Lack, clasping his own behind his back and strolling among the lab tables, "may have a little trouble with today's dissection. For this subpopulation I have one piece of advice." He gathers the moment. "Get over it," he says.

Leah watches the point of the scalpel whisper across Angeline's wrist.

"Get over it, people," says Mr. Lack. "Be glad the frogs

are dead. In my day, we pithed our frogs." He holds an invisible needle high in the air and stirs.

Angeline dips her head. "That's the eighth plague," she says behind a curtain of hair. "Pithing frogs."

Rana Fegrina is larger than Leah expected; he is nearly the size of her hand, with limbs extended in full leap. Did he die this way, or did they flatten him under a book? Most of his green has drained away. Chlorophyll, Leah thinks stupidly, as Mr. Lack turns and strolls down her aisle.

"And any girl who utters the words 'Eew, it's so gross,' regardless of intonation, loses ten points," says Mr. Lack. He wheels around, guided by sonar. "Boys lose twenty-five," he snaps. "And Miss Yost, please desist from the dissection of your own hand."

Angeline lowers the scalpel until it is the merest inch above the lab table. Then she drops it. It sounds like a tiny piece of glass breaking.

"Miss Yost joins us for the second year," says Mr. Lack.

The top of Leah's head bursts into flame. She takes another step back. Angeline spreads her fingers, revealing a small red smear in the vicinity of her lifeline. Then she hides it in her fist.

"Open your kits," says Mr. Lack, "pin the frog, and decide which among you shall make the first cut."

Leah is now standing four feet from her partner. It won't do. She steps closer to Angeline. Rana Fegrina, on his back on the dissection tray, stares up at her through the blind eye of his belly.

"I'll pin if you cut," whispers Leah, looking at the frog instead of at Angeline.

· "I cut last year," says Angeline.

Angeline's voice has exactly the same drape as her hair. Leah can't tell if she's being ironic. Also, she has never stood this close to a slut. She thought a slut would have yellow teeth. She wants to check Angeline's teeth and rifle her backpack for notes and pierce the curtain of hair with her finger, as if breaking the sleek vane of a feather. She wants to say: Is it true?

"I'll do absolutely everything if you just cut," says Leah, frantic. As a sign of good faith she plucks up the first pin and positions it over Rana Fegrina's gray-green palm. She has to duck her head so she won't see it break the skin. Instead she concentrates on Angeline Yost's bellbottoms. They are perfect, these bellbottoms. They clump over Angeline's sneakers in front, and in back they're frayed from being stood on. The jeans taper and flare as if they had been breathed onto Angeline Yost by God.

Leah counts to twenty for each of the four pins, two for the hands and two for the feet. Rana Fegrina does not struggle.

"Look at him," says Angeline. "He died for your sins. You know what's weird about frogs?"

"Are you going to cut?" says Leah. Her voice is a handkerchief fluttering on a twig. She clears her throat. She wonders if there is such a thing as pushing Angeline too far.

"What's weird about frogs," says Angeline, "is they only recognize food when it moves. You set a dead fly in front of a frog, he'll fucking starve."

Leah imagines Rana Fegrina crouched before his dinner—a fly sizzling on a tiny white plate, size of a fingernail.

Rana Fegrina secretes an ancient green wisdom through his pores. Rana Fegrina knows that time is a circle. Rana Fegrina knows that all things will pass. Rana Fegrina knows that sometimes a girl has to wait in the hall because her father is going to the bathroom in his bed. Rana Fegrina knows where the love goes when the body dies. The frog's thoughts coil along his hidden tongue, deadly as a bullwhip.

Leah decides to attempt a string of sentences.

"My mother's like that," she says. "She only recognizes food when it has no calories." She wants to stop but it's too late. "If you put a cake in front of my mother she'd starve too."

Angeline picks up the scissors in her right hand and, with the tweezers in her left, nips up the skin above Rana Fegrina's groin. She doesn't read the directions; she's done this before.

"That's just dieting. That's nothing," says Angeline. She wrinkles her nose, jabs a scissor-blade into the pickled skin and snips, unzipping the body cavity. "A girl in my building, her mama keeps a padlock on the fridge."

The heart of Rana Fegrina is a five-chambered thing. Three chambers have walls like the webbing between Rana's toes: the sinus venosus, the right auricle and the left auricle. But two chambers are muscled like a father's bicep: the ventricle and the truncus arteriosus.

The heart of Rana Fegrina contains doors that open in one direction only.

The heart of Rana Fegrina cannot be broken. It can only be stopped.

＆

What Leah suddenly notices, as she unsettles the liver with her probe and exposes the tiny purse of a gall bladder, is how Angeline leans in so close that crabs could even now be leaping from her hair to Leah's. She imagines the crabs as a matrix of tiny translucent spiders so that if she were to actually look, Angeline Yost's pubes and scalp might appear to be a moving, shimmering mass.

She holds her breath.

"God, how do they get all these organs in one friggin' frog," says Angeline.

Leah wonders if disgust is not that different from awe. She prods the gall bladder, marks it on her labsheet. She says, "I think it's kind of beautiful."

"You need a doctor," says Angeline.

"I just mean—" The probe trembles. She tucks the gall bladder back into its bed between the lobes. "I just mean the frog has everything it needs to be a frog," says Leah.

"You need an ambulance," says Angeline.

"No, listen," says Leah, desperate to make sense. What is it her mother says? A perfect room has everything it needs and nothing else; it has a fireplace and a sofa and good lighting—but this is nothing Angeline would want to hear.

Angeline smirks. It is a sound she makes in her nose. "Have it your way," she says.

Leah looks at the wreckage that is Rana Fegrina, the flaps of belly-skin spread and pinned, the tumble of innards unspooled. She thinks of her jewelry box, dumped out on her bed.

"Ugly-beautiful," says Leah.

"Huh," says Angeline.

Leah nudges a small nugget with the probe, holds it there in case Angeline wants to see. But Angeline is looking into the cup of her palm. "Kidney?" says Leah.

"Look, don't wait for me," says Angeline. The edge of her knife is in her voice. Leah understands suddenly that the knife is a thing deep inside Angeline; it is not a thing you would find in her sock.

Leah withdraws the probe. She slides her labsheet into a central position on the table, where she has to reach over somewhat to write. On the sheet is a mimeographed drawing of Rana, splayed and radiating lines from the organs. At the end of each line is another line for the organ's name. Leah has filled in most of hers.

Pancreas, she writes.

When Angeline copies she could be filling in a grocery list. Her handwriting is all elbows and knees and she seems only vaguely aware that the words relate to the picture. She drops the *r* from pancreas. The red smear in her palm stays hidden as she writes, a stain in the chamber of a shell.

"I could help you," Leah says.

"You missed stuff," says Angeline, pushing the labsheet toward Leah with the eraser end of her pencil.

Ureter. Cloaca.

"I could," says Leah. "For the final." Because now she sees something inside herself as clearly as she sees the knife in Angeline: one single ability, the classification of living things, that could maybe save a person's life. Angeline calls to her from under the waves, and she, Leah, walks into the water. Angeline sits alone and wide-legged on the south ledge after lunch, and Leah is the one who stops, extends a pack of Winstons. Other kids glance at them but they are safe in a fold of shadow, and Leah believes it is the shadow of Keith. Angeline saying, *You'll get a reputation if you hang with me*. Angeline saying: *I never had a friend like you.*

"Give it up," says Angeline, her writing hand still in a nautilus around the pencil. "I got a D on the midterm."

Angeline whispering: *The whole hot dog thing, Dierdre started that, it was all a big lie.*

"I could tutor you," says Leah. "For nothing. I could get you a B."

She watches Angeline yank the pins from Rana Fegrina, uninstructed, and walk across the room with the tray. She watches Rana Fegrina slide into the trash as if he never lived. She wonders what the body releases when it dies; she wonders if there is something she has forgotten to say.

"Wake up," says Angeline. "It's next fucking Wednesday."

It takes Leah a minute to realize they are still talking about the final. She tries to look Angeline in the eye. She almost gets there, but the machinery stops when she is looking at Angeline's mouth.

Angeline saying, *Trust me*. Her breath sweet.

"I could do it," Leah says. "After school. I just have to go home first."

This is not exactly true. The apartment is empty. Her mother will wait in a green vinyl hospital chair with a book on French furniture until they take away her husband's tray. Leah goes home every day and cleans her room because it is a thing she has to do. She works from a list of rotating jobs—burnish desk with lemon oil, dust behind books, line books up like teeth along edge of shelf, clean inside bureau drawers, re-fold the underwear. By Saturday morning her room quivers like a heart in its new skin so that she is afraid to touch anything.

Angeline looks at the ceiling as if seeking patience in the perforated tile. The movement slides the blunt gold edge of her hair down to the bone-wings on her back. Then she starts writing a number on a corner of Leah's labsheet. Leah yanks it away. A green film glides down over Angeline's expression like the secret eyelid of a cat.

"He'll make me do it over," Leah says.

They are not allowed to have notebooks at the lab tables. Leah pushes up her sleeve. Angeline Yost is halfway through the ballpoint tattoo of her home address when Leah detects it—the small, sharp tang of seaweed and salt.

Low tide.

She filters it through her memory.

It is the smell of seaweed thirsting on the sand; it is the smell of the horseshoe crab's shell after the crab has been returned to the physical universe.

It is the smell of Rana Fegrina, disemboweled for her sins.

It is the smell of Phisohex after the patient has been bathed—sponged and rolled and patted dry behind the curtain by a nurse in sympathetic shoes, a nurse who talks as if tending a frightened child.

It is gray ammonia sloshed from an orderly's yellow

bucket, it is the Sea Breeze her mother strokes onto her father's slackening neck.

It is the smell of the body releasing. It is a tinge of lemony sweat.

It is the smell of B.O., though Leah cannot be certain whether it is Angeline's or her own, and Whitman is wrong: the atmosphere is a perfume. It tastes of the distillation. She is in love with it, it is the beating of her heart.

Normal People Don't Live Like This

Helen Levinson stared into her daughter's top drawer, seeking folded white cotton. Instead: a tangle of fuscia bikinis. Satin brassieres in a psychedelic print—psychedelic, one of those Jimi Hendrix drug words.

Fishnet stockings, parrot-green.

With one finger she lifted the tumbled underwear. She saw a cloisonne bracelet, a pretend-Pucci halter top. She saw earrings made with peacock feathers, the eyes irridescent with unblinking knowledge. And there was white, all right—a ransacked package of Kent cigarettes, and several price tags, still attached to the underthings by pins.

Yesterday Leah left for school in a cotton blouse that Helen had ironed, and came home late wearing the Pucci top and peacock earrings, allegedly borrowed from Pansy Prideau. This morning she tried to wear the stockings to school, but Helen blocked the bedroom doorway.

"Not fishnet, for Chrissake," Leah said, peeling them off. "Windowpane. Jesus. All the girls wear windowpanes."

She turned up the volume on her red transistor radio. "Down in New Orleans," she sang, her voice ribbon-thin but her chin high, as if this was a place she had passed some time but that Helen would never see.

"Girls do not wear stockings, Leah, they wear *socks*," Helen said. "And don't swear."

"Oly wears stockings," Leah announced. "Pansy wears stockings. Angeline Yost wears goddamn stockings."

"Really?" Helen had never heard of this Angeline person. "Do they match her diaphragm?"

Leah looked shocked, then delighted. "No," she said, with lofty amusement. She hoisted her backpack, unclean object from the army surplus, and gathered it to her chest as she stalked to the door—not wanting, Helen sensed, to fracture the moment by struggling into the straps. The front door had almost closed when Helen saw it catch on the white toe of a Ked. Leah stuck her head back in.

"For your information," she said, "Angeline Yost is on the goddamn pill."

Helen wanted to slap Miss Somebody across the face. Instead she turned off the radio, opened her pocketbook and tucked in the halter top, the earrings, the fishnet windowpanes. On her way out later that morning she nodded at the doorman. One-bedroom apartment with an airshaft view—the doorman was a point of pride.

Now she had the dark apartment but no husband. She had three good skirt-suits from Bonwit's and a Pauline Trigere coat, but no husband. She had a pearl choker that she wore to work. She had a man's wedding ring in a drawer, folded in tissue, and thirty thousand life-insurance in a savings account—untouched, except for those suits.

She had a daughter who seemed to be smoking and stealing and dressing underneath like a prostitute, who wrote in a secret notebook with tight slanted script, one arm curled protectively around the page.

She had a recurring fantasy of being struck by a bus. The bus would knock her into a coma for many days. All she'd have to do was breathe.

She had the clipped walk of a person who pared herself to the essentials: muscle, bone, an eye for quality, calcium tablets for the nails, one pair of pumps, polished. Helen headed east on 88th, turned left. Her calves flashed under the navy skirt. She stopped at the building where the Prideau girls lived.

Helen knew this: Every room needed a touch of black. A picture frame. A vase. Some queen-of-night tulips, if you could find the rare florist who knew from chrysanthemums. Black lent definition to a space. It made the edges crisp.

But Mrs. Prideau did not believe in just a touch, Helen could see that walking in. Her turtleneck, her jeans, her hightop sneakers for heaven's sake—all black. The cross that hung from her silver chain: onyx, brimming with ink. Helen glanced past her and spotted a black coffee table, black sofa. And a black butterfly chair, with that ungainly canvas seat.

"I'm Leah's mother," she said. "Helen. I hope you'll excuse me, just showing up."

Mrs. Prideau held a cigarette in one hand and a red pencil in the other. She tipped her head to one side with interest.

"I'm Bonita," she said, opening the door wide. "You have a good daughter. Smart. Come in."

Bonita, that meant pretty, but this woman had hair short as a man's. Her lips were carmine, the same color that bloomed at the end of her cigarette, but her eyes were bare. Not even mascara, which would be so easy—really, there was no excuse. Helen had Blackglama hair. She wore mascara, lipstick and Estée Lauder foundation powder, always. She regarded powder as an item of decency, like the wearing of underclothes. She followed Bonita into a miasma of smoke.

"Happy is the house that shelters a friend." Bonita waved at the butterfly chair and took her place gingerly on the sofa, which was layered with typed papers. "Emerson," she said, folding her legs beneath her.

What was the implication—that Helen's small apartment had somehow failed to harbor friends? The typed papers made her think of college, of girls with books fastened lightly to their hips, laughing in clusters.

"George Nelson," said Helen, changing the subject, nodding at the coffee table. She lowered herself into the butterfly, felt herself slung in the canvas, trapped.

"Nooo, I'm sure it was Ralph Waldo," said Bonita.

"Your table," said Helen. "All those black slats. It's by George Nelson. It's a good piece."

"Good?" Bonita looked at the table appraisingly, as if it

had just ankled in on its own. "I didn't know it had a name," she said. "My girls found it on the street."

Her girls, Oleander and Pansy, never came to visit Leah; it was always Leah over here. *Happy is the house that shelters a friend.* Helen felt her purse sitting rigid on her lap, pregnant with evidence.

"Speaking of your girls," said Helen, "if you and your husband ever go for overnights, I'd be glad to take them." This was not true. She was sure they wouldn't say a word to her; they would smirk, and close Leah's door; they would leave the fridge ajar. Still, it was the warmest overture she could think to make. "It would be a pleasure," she said. "Leah spends half her life here."

Bonita glanced toward a closed door and smiled. Her smile had a twist at one end, as if Helen had offered her a slice of lemon. "Overnights, my goodness," said Bonita. "My husband and I wouldn't walk to the corner together. He's never here anyway. If I want to visit a friend, I leave the girls alone. They're fine."

Helen placed both hands on her pocketbook. Alone? And what did it mean, *visit a friend?* "You don't worry they'll get in trouble?"

"You must be kidding." Bonita stood and stretched, rolling her shoulders up and back, unselfconscious as a cat. "My girls are already in trouble," she said. "A little supervision is not going to help. You'll have coffee, won't you? I need to caffeinate like you can't believe."

Helen followed Bonita's narrow back and broad hips into a kitchen that appeared to have exploded. Pots nested crazily on the stove. Boxes of Lucky Charms and Trix on the counter, open, the waxed bags gaping, and boxes of mix for macaroni and cheese, and a bag of chocolate chip cookies, and diet pills. *Two* boxes of diet pills, both torn open, and a refrigerator flapping with pages from the fashion magazines. Helen tried to avert her eyes but there was no escaping the detritus, the empty bottles of Coca-Cola, a jar of red pencils, a notebook, two butter knives encrusted with sandwich residue.

Why hadn't Leah said anything? She knew normal people didn't live like this.

"I usually have a full pot up," said Bonita, "working at home."

"Are you a writer?" said Helen. She was careful not to lean against any surface; she barely knew where to stand.

"Book doctor." Bonita shook grounds out of the percolator into the full sink, rinsed it under a thin trickle of hot.

The faucet needed a super, it needed a plumber, the entire kitchen needed a Dumpster. Helen waited for Bonita to say: *And you, what do you do?* But Bonita probably thought she was a housewife. Helen groped for another question.

"Books get sick?"

The family needed a psychiatrist. And this apartment— almost beyond salvation. This apartment needed a decorator. Yes.

"Oh, you should see the current patient," said Bonita. "Downright feverish."

And just like that, Helen saw it: Bonita Prideau's kitchen, counters cleared and sparkling, a Christmas cactus hanging in the window, full flower. The walls yellow—a warm, English-library yellow, Benjamin Moore 311. Then the cabinet doors: a high-gloss black.

"I guess I'm kind of a room doctor," said Helen. "I'm a decorator. In training," she added. "I'll be on staff in six months."

Plates crashed in the sink while Bonita rummaged. She pulled out matching cups, an unexpected harmony that caught Helen's attention, and washed them under the trickle.

"Decorator in training, huh," said Bonita. "I swear Oly would rather starve than wash a dish—is it like that at your house?" She surveyed the countertops, then swiped the flowered mugs on her jeans.

"No," said Helen.

Bonita looked at her. "I guess it wouldn't be," she said. She packed coffee into the percolator, dialed on the gas, struck a match. "Eliot has a lovely line about a cup of strength," she said, adjusting the flame. "I like to think she meant coffee. How do you take it?"

Helen considered the various facets of this question.

"Before you answer," said Bonita, "smell the milk, would you?"

Helen tugged at the chrome handle on the refrigerator. The door gasped open and she shivered, not from cold but because the head of iceberg was unwrapped, and a package of hot dogs, sliced open, leaked onto a shelf. She handed the open milk carton to Bonita, who sniffed it, looked away as if listening for distant music, then set it on the counter.

"Okay," said Bonita. "Just supposing. How *would* you resuscitate this rat hole?"

Throw it all out, everything, Helen wanted to say. But then Bonita might shutter her gray irises and this highly tentative friendship would go up in a smoke-headache, which Helen was in fact developing. She could think of twenty ways to resuscitate this rat hole. Indeed, Bonita could be her first client. A friend-client. No fee, of course. Just a reasonable outlay for lamps, fabric, paint, followed by surprise, pleasure, appreciation—

"First I have to know what you love," said Helen, and felt her toes curl as if into warm sand. "Just because a room is beautiful to me doesn't mean you would find it so." Gray Alistair, her employer, always began with exactly these words, though he was wrong, a well-decorated room was a fact of beauty, indisputable, the way a rose was indisputable. No one could argue that a rose was not beautiful.

Bonita carried both cups into the living room and set them directly on the George Nelson table, without benefit of saucer. "What I love," she said, and tipped her head again, as if letting all the thoughts collect on one side.

"I love honesty in all things," she said at last. "I love my typewriter. I love coffee cups and ashtrays, I really do. I love having my girls' friends come over and hearing them laugh. I love the way a leather wallet feels after you've had it about fifteen years, do you know? And I love wearing black. It's so sensual, don't you think?"

Helen did not think. Not one of these things had ever crossed her mind.

"I mean," she said, after a respectful pause, "how you'd love a room to look."

"Oh, I don't know. I'd like a room of my own, though, if you could arrange that." Bonita laughed. "A clean, well-lighted place. What do you think? I share a bedroom with the girls, I'm sure Leah's told you. My husband has the other one." She narrowed her eyes. "A New York divorce," she said. "We can't afford two rents."

Helen struggled not to register shock. These children see too much, she thought. A woman should sleep in her husband's bed. "It must be crowded for you."

"God, is it crowded," said Bonita. "I share a bed with Oleander. She talks in her sleep. About boys, I'm sure. I literally dream about finding a secret room."

Helen stared. "You do? I've had that dream a hundred times."

"With hallways," said Bonita. "And extra bathrooms."

"Foyers," said Helen. "Bedrooms. A big kitchen." She squeezed her shoulders together, a tiny tremor. "Once I dreamed a ballroom," she said, and stopped. Maybe Bonita would admit to the rest of it. The part where stairs funneled into basements. Where seeping pipes snaked along the ceiling. Where metal doors rasped open onto black shaftways, and refused to close.

"Must be an archetype," said Bonita coolly.

Disappointed, Helen leaned forward, which in the butterfly chair was more like folding herself up. She took an earnest sip of coffee. "What do you hate?"

"Excuse me?" said Bonita. "You ask such interesting questions. Why?"

"Some people have passionate dislikes," said Helen. "You might hate wall-to-wall carpeting. You might hate green. I'd need to know." If she was lucky, Bonita would hate her present curtains; they were mauve, nubby, and short.

"Ahh." Bonita didn't need to tip her head this time. "Hate is so much more interesting than love, isn't it? I hate a room without books. I hate a desk without papers. I hate not having a cat, but I'm allergic. I hate the way laundry piles up around here. We all share clothes, so nobody feels that the laundry is exactly *theirs*, do you know? I hate that Pansy—" Bonita laughed. It was a tight, hard sound. "But I'm not giving you anything useful, I'm sure."

In her softest voice, Helen said: "Pansy what?"

"Oh, Pansy's lost." Bonita sucked on her cigarette. "I know where she *is*, give or take a few subway stops. But she's lost."

Happy is the house, thought Helen. She wondered if *lost* was a condition involving halter tops and fishnet window-panes, being left to her own devices while her mother *visited a friend*.

"You probably think I hate color," Bonita said, "but the truth is I just don't want it touching my skin. Does that sound neurotic to you?"

"No," said Helen. Because, strangely, it didn't. She felt suddenly powerful. "Bonita," she said, "we could do this. Listen. Bookshelves along that wall. We could buy them unfinished and ebonize them—stain them black. Then *café au lait* walls. We could paint them ourselves. And black enamel baseboards."

Bonita shook her head, but Helen rushed on. "We could do floor cushions in red, and long red curtains. Do you have a desk?"

"You're very good," said Bonita. "Café-au-lait walls—you're really very good. Let's not and say we did. More coffee?"

Helen blinked. She had not yet come to the Indian fabric panels, tenting and separating the beds.

"But it's easy," she said. "It's just fabric and paint."

"I can't afford it," said Bonita, assessing her last half-inch of cigarette, "and if you keep going it'll always be there, haunting my mind."

Helen wanted to touch Bonita on the arm and say, *But listen.* She felt like she was crossing a river on a bridge that stopped halfway. She decided to take one more step out.

"If you have a beautiful home," she said, "you can have a beautiful life. I really believe that."

Bonita stubbed the cigarette out hard. Helen glanced at the pack: it said Kent. "You may find this hard to believe," said Bonita, "but I am perversely satisfied with my life."

Helen cradled her coffee cup in both palms. "I could do it with you," she said, rocking forward and back. "I could do it *for* you," and realized too late that she had run out of bridge, that she was not offering a gift at all but asking for one, and that Bonita knew this.

"It's a generous thought," said Bonita. "You'll find another place."

In the bus fantasy, Helen awakened days later in the hospital. Sometimes she was about ten years old, and sometimes she was her real age. People gathered at her bed, their hands resting lightly upon her ankles, her shoulders. The people wore white and bent gently toward her face.

Helen opened her purse with a low click. She talked with a new voice that seemed to come from the polished pocketbook. "I'm taking up your day," she said. "I'm sorry. I came to return Pansy's things. At least Leah said they were Pansy's. I was hoping you could tell me."

Bonita stopped her coffee cup halfway to her lips and smiled. "I knew there was a reason," she said. "Ante up."

Helen pulled out the fake-Pucci halter top and draped it across the George Nelson slats as if Bonita might care to purchase it. "It's obviously a copy."

"It looks like a real top to me," said Bonita. "I've seen this. Things come and go around here. You sure it isn't Leah's?"

"Leah gets three dollars a week," said Helen, "and I buy her clothes."

"*Really*," said Bonita.

"Well, yes," said Helen. "Don't you?"

"Their tastes keep changing, don't you find? So no, I don't. I give them ten dollars every six months and they go to thrift shops."

"Used clothes?" Helen could not imagine wearing strangers' old clothes. She did not even want strangers polishing her toenails.

Bonita plucked at her turtleneck. "Fifty cents," she said. "Cashmere. It's hard to beat."

Helen set out the peacock earrings. "Leah said these are Pansy's too."

"Things float around," said Bonita dreamily. She picked up an earring and stroked the splines of the feather.

Helen nodded as though she heard this all the time, this absence of boundaries between mothers and daughers.

"Frankly," she said, "I was afraid Leah might be shoplifting."

Bonita held a feather to her earlobe, raised her brows. "Should I go pierced? My girls keep telling me."

My girls, like they were a flock of tumbling puppies.

"But if they're Pansy's," said Helen.

"If they are, she probably stole them herself. But I'll ask." Bonita lit another cigarette and rested her head on the back of the sofa to exhale. "If Leah's stealing, she'll outgrow it. God knows I did. Girls try all sorts of stunts at this age. It passes." Her gaze traveled across the ceiling. "I hope," she added.

Helen looked into her black coffee and wondered which part of the cup had rubbed against Bonita's jeans. "I don't think I share your tolerance for stunts," she said lightly. "Would you give Pansy back her things?" She added the stockings to the pile for good measure, and snapped her purse shut.

"Uh-oh," said Bonita. "I blew it, huh?"

The smoke in the room had an edge now, like a chisel. It hurt Helen's head. She was sure her clothes would have an odor. They would smell like the inside of a thrift shop on a rainy day.

"Don't leave yet," said Bonita. "It's been nice. And I need to ask you something."

"Anything." Helen felt suddenly revived. She hoped Bonita had a question or confession that might bind them, over future visits and many cups of strength, into a loose friendship. *Pansy is smoking, Oleander is drinking, I think my husband is having—*

"It's about writing, actually. I've got this writer," said Bonita, "who thinks he's Hemingway in bed. Remember that business with Maria when the earth moves?"

Helen, from the depths of the butterfly chair, said: "Maria?"

"When Robert Jordan asks if she felt the earth move." Bonita scanned a sheaf of pages, their margins loopy with red pencil, like broken capillaries. "And Maria says"—she clapped a hand passionately to her chest—"Yes, as I died." The hand waved dismissively. "It's almost Victorian, don't you think? Or French. *La petit mort.* So my publisher gives me this overwrought manuscript, same macho drivel, but tells me don't get too violent with it."

Bonita raised her eyebrows into scoops, as if to confirm some mutual understanding. Then she read aloud a long passage of physical entanglement involving pine needles and the frequent rearrangement of limbs, something felt violently in a person's marrow, and ending, after a kind of seizure, with the word *convulsed.*

"Helen," said Bonita, "is that for real, or is that a load of crap?"

Helen stared at her. A woman, talking like that.

"I'm not asking about the writing," said Bonita. "I'm asking if that's how it feels."

Helen tried to focus. What was it about marrow? She loved the promising snap of a thin bone, if she was alone in the kitchen.

"How *what* feels," she said, to make absolutely sure she

did not answer the wrong question. Perhaps she would start with a delicate euphemism. At some point she might simply have to leave.

"For God's sake," said Bonita, "having a climax. You don't *convulse*, do you?"

Absurdly, Helen thought of sugar melting and Champagne fizzing, and she was trying to find nonculinary words for this simultaneous reduction and overflow, words that would show equal parts womanly knowledge and feminine restraint, when she heard them: Bonita's girls. First the muffled whomp of a metal door opening, then the crack of a doorknob, probably dented, smacking a wall, plaster. Then a voice, low and velvety, saying *I call the Trix*, and a second voice with higher, floral notes saying *You mean you turn tricks*.

Then a flash of laughter. It was brittle and bright, a wine glass tinkling into shards.

Helen knew that laugh.

Three girls, one of them hers, spilled into the living room and stopped, seeing company.

"Hi," said Oleander, after just a tick of hesitation, and drifted toward the sofa where her mother sat.

Pansy flashed a glance at Helen, dropped her bookbag to the floor—they all carried those slovenly army packs, Helen noted—and headed for the kitchen. When she emerged she was moving slowly, carrying the box of Trix and taking in the merchandise spread on the George Nelson table.

"Cool earrings," said Pansy. She looked straight at Helen. She stood in her own home, such as it was, wearing a scoop-neck top cut lower than anything Helen had ever owned. She had the full chest of a woman. "Yours?" she said.

"Yours, allegedly," said Helen. She glanced at her daughter, who was chewing on a coil of pumpkin-colored hair.

Bonita laughed. "I guess that settles that."

"For real?" Pansy didn't wait for an answer. Without removing her gold hoops, she threaded the peacock earrings through her lobes. Then, instead of going off to find a mirror, she leaned against the wall, buried her hand in the cereal box, and studied the two mothers quizzically, as if waiting for them to sing.

Helen's watch read twelve-twenty. School must be out for lunch.

"We were talking about decorating," she said.

"Oh, good." Oleander rifled the package of Kents. A small badge of skin glinted near her wrist, reminding Helen of an old story, an attack with a cigarette in junior high. Thank God they had sent Leah private for two years. And there was a looseness to Oly's body that Helen mistrusted; it made her think of midnight rooftops, of walks that veered erratically into the park.

"Cause this place is a rat hole," Oly said. She wormed an orange plastic lighter from her jeans pocket, lit up, and ejected a fat, milky ring that shivered and dissolved.

"Why?" said Helen. "Why is it a rat hole, Oleander?"

Oly shrugged: one shoulder, half her mouth.

"Because," said Helen, "it doesn't have to be."

And then Leah, edging closer, made a slight movement. It was over almost before it began, and yet Helen perceived it, a kind of slippage, a reflex of the fingers and eyes. It was the move of a smoker, reaching.

Caught, Leah vacated her expression. Her face was a pewter cup, empty and cool.

Leap. What was it Leo used to say? *Leap, and the net will appear.*

"Don't let me stop you," said Helen.

Leah widened her eyes. The green in her irises turned translucent, bottomless. "Scuse me?" Her voice had a nap to it, like velvet.

"Don't lie to me," said Helen. "Go ahead. Smoke."

Leah shook her head, a tiny vibration.

"Do it," said Helen. "Do whatever it is you do."

"Mom. Stop it."

She was lost and she was not lost. She stole fishnet windowpanes but she peeled them off. She was Helen's and she was not Helen's, this redheaded stalk.

"I will not stop," said Helen. "I'm your mother. Have your cigarette. Let's get this out in the open."

Pansy and Oleander had lovely noses, flaring and flat, exactly like Bonita's. They had mouths like rosebuds. They look like dolls, thought Helen, pretty ones, with staring glass eyes. The bad girls always look like dolls.

"I *don't smoke*," said Leah.

"Oh, crap," said Pansy, amiably.

Helen looked to Bonita for some wry editorial comment, but Bonita was preoccupied. She seemed to be peering at Pansy's arms.

On the skin: a long row of red lines, carved razor-straight. One, apparently new, was encrusted with amber, the skin around it swollen. Helen looked back at Bonita and saw in her eyes a familiar irony, metallic, but also sad, and beneath that a letting-go, a relinquishing, as if Pansy were sliding slowly off a roof.

She's dreamed it all, thought Helen. The basement, the snaking pipes, shaftways with doors that do not close.

Leah dropped her bookbag. She knelt by the coffee table. She dug a cigarette from the rumpled pack and stuck out her hand, waiting. Not even needing to *ask*, thought Helen, amazed. Not even looking up. Just knowing that Oly would place in her palm the orange lighter.

Which Oly did, her glance at Helen oblique, as if from under a veil.

The understanding between these girls filled Helen with wonder. Even in high school, with her own best friends, she had never known anything like it.

"What do you mean, it doesn't have to be like this?" said Oly.

Leah's lower lip, nearly as pale as her skin, curled as she exhaled. The exhalation was a sigh; it was the end of thirst.

"Oleander," said Helen, "it's really very simple." What trespass, she thought. Lecturing Bonita's girls. But Bonita was tuned in to another station. The only sound was the rasp of cereal, Pansy's hand deep in the box, stirring.

"You do the laundry," said Helen, emboldened, staring back at Oly. "You clean the kitchen. When you take off a blouse, you hang it up. You treat your home with respect, the way you'd want to be treated yourself."

"That's my halter top," said Leah, though she made no move to claim it.

Normal People Don't Live like This :: 79

Pansy stopped stirring. Her enamel eyes were focused on Helen.

"What if you treat yourself like shit?" she said.

"Pansy," said Bonita. Her voice seemed to come from another room.

Pansy turned the lacquered gaze on her mother, as if Bonita were a specimen struggling under a pin.

"Pansy. Honey," Bonita said. Her fingers moved as if magnetized to the hollow between her collarbones.

Leah, kneeling at the coffee table, did not look up. But Helen knew she felt it: the way a mother's gaze settles softly on a daughter's hair and shoulders, like a fine, floating shawl. It was not a shawl that had ever landed on Helen, yet she knew it by its absence, knew how to send it wafting where her hands could not go.

Leah scissored the cigarette between two fingers. She lifted it to her lips. She inhaled like a person drinking from a tall glass on a hot day. Then she arched her neck and sent out a stream of smoke. Her body shuddered briefly.

It will hold, Helen thought. She was not lost. She was merely trying all sorts of stunts. Leah Sophia, one name from each grandmother. The cigarette was nothing. It was only smoke. It was only a moment: daughter, fifteen.

Underwater

It *rises to completion* like a sun within the egg.

Some scientist wrote that. Leopold Auerbach, like a million years ago. Eighteen-something. Leah sees him storklike, rabbinical, the ocular of his microscope imprinting a ring around his eye. Muscle cramps to stone between Leopold's shoulders as he presides over holy union of sperm and egg.

Leopold forgets he is thirsty. He forgets he is married. He hears cytoplasm ticking. He walks the labyrinth of the thumbprint of God. For ninety lost minutes he watches the pronuclei fuse. Vacuoles, he calls them— they didn't have pronuclei then. He gropes for a gold pen, gift from his father, and his handwriting travels off the page as he stares at the dawning nucleus. *It rises to completion.* Leah has read it. She reads a lot of stuff they don't assign.

But this is not a thing to say, not now, with Angeline weeping on the edge of the tub. Angeline is a junior and

Leah is a nobody. Angeline is the most silvery person Leah has ever known. Her voice, her hair, her skin, even the narrow light of suspicion she casts from her eyes, all silver. Angeline is the moon.

"Why won't it just *die?*" says Angeline. "How do I make it die?"

Leah wonders why she has been brought here, into the locked bathroom of some guy named Jay, to answer this specific question. Maybe it's a trick question. She says, "Have an abortion?"

Through the bathroom door she hears the twelve ringing strings of Jay's guitar. Jay can play everything Neil Young plays, and he has Neil Young's hair, too. He has a ladderback chair hanging crooked on the living room wall. Leah couldn't believe no one was bothering to fix it, so she straightened it on its nail. You yardarm, said Jay, you don't get it, and made her tip it to the left again. It felt like she was pulling her own rib out of skew. She has no idea what a yardarm is.

"Look, I don't have anyone else to ask." Angeline's face is a crumple of peony, disarranged from crying. She touches Leah on the hand and looks right into her. "You're my best friend." Her fingertips streaming light. "You couldn't loan me a hundred and fifty dollars, could you?"

Leah's hand burns where Angeline's fingers rest upon it in a light chord. "I wish."

This is five-sixths a lie, because she has a hundred and eighteen dollars, right now, in her backpack. It has taken more than a year to save, all ones and fives snicked from her mother's polished purse. She keeps the money rolled in a makeup case—untouched, because most of what she wants, she steals. Earrings, cigarettes, magazines. It occurs to her that placing the bills in Angeline's palm would constitute an unforgettable act of rescue, allowing Leah to rise to completion in this very bathroom.

"What about the father?" she says.

"It's Graham," says Angeline, morose.

"Oh," says Leah. Graham is the Central Park boyfriend. He was hanging out at Bethesda Fountain, dealing a little pot and watching Angeline sunbathe. Leah waits for enlightenment, but Angeline just smokes. "Why can't Graham pay for it?"

"Don't you remember anything?" says Angeline. "I *told* you. His best friend is a talent scout."

Leah remembers something about an audition. It keeps not materializing. It's a sensitive subject. She doesn't get the connection but she better not ask. After a respectful moment she says, "What about Jack?"

Jack is a New York City truancy officer. He always uses a rubber.

"Jack's got three kids," says Angeline, waving her cigarette dismissively. "He never has a hundred and fifty dollars. What're you, kidding?"

Leah loves Angeline. But occasionally she feels as if Angeline has backed her up to a wall and is siphoning air out of her lungs with a rubber tube. This is one of those times. She can't yank the tube out because she is Angeline's best friend. She shouldn't even *want* to yank it out. For one wild second she imagines bolting into the street and getting hit by a cab. But then Angeline would notice she wasn't in school. Angeline would stand too close to the hospital bed, making challenging statements that end in "What're you, kidding?" and fingering the intravenous line.

Sometimes after school, though, Angeline takes a deep hit of pot, holds it in her lungs, and issues riveting dispatches in a tight, non-breathing voice using words like *blow job* and *ball*. At those moments Leah is in ecstacy. Plus Angeline thinks Leah is smart. This chick gets A's in fuckin' everything, she tells people, and Leah glows as if Angeline has put a match to her. She has been chosen. They are *best friends*.

"Look, you're the science freak," says Angeline, and the word *freak* glides splinterlike under Leah's skin. "There's gotta be something I can take."

"Take?"

Angeline has other friends, but they are the wrong kind of freak for her particular problem. They are juniors too. They mix vodka with Tab and drink it at lunch. Then they take white crosses so they won't zone out. Everyone sees them on the south ledge, laughing too loudly and prodding each other in the ribs, watching the parade of fools. Everyone sees them. Sometimes in bio Angeline says *you gonna eat with us or what?* and each time Leah has to study, but when they are alone together Angeline is a knife under folds of silk and Leah can't look away.

"Drain cleaner," says Angeline. "Bleach. All that shit under the sink."

Leah sucks air in through her teeth. Maybe Jay is wondering why they are locked in the bathroom, and he will look at them funny, after. Jay is Angeline's friend. He is twenty-three. He is not a boyfriend but sometimes they ball. Jay has a mole on the side of his cock. He delivers mattresses from a white no-name truck and on Saturday and Sunday he plays guitar and sings in the park. When Angeline sings with him they can pull down thirty, forty bucks. Pull down, how Angeline says it. She gets a third. The whole thing, the ease of it, makes Leah insanely envious.

"Don't even think about it," says Leah. "Poison works on the mother first." This sounds right; it sounds like something a nurse would say. "How late are you, anyway?"

"How late? What do you, fucking keep *track?*"

Leah waits this one out. The tiny attacks just dissipate, she has found, if she holds very still.

"Oh my God." Angeline sits up straight on the edge of the tub, one hand over her belly. "You could punch me in the stomach."

"Uterus," says Leah, grateful for familiar turf. Gingerly she slides Angeline's hand about four inches down, careful not to touch anything but wrist—else Angeline might call her a *sick sister*. She imagines Angeline's uterus as a pulpy glove, and in the palm of the glove lies a dark, beating fish.

Angeline presses, thoughtfully. "You punch me there I'll pee."

"I'm not punching you there," says Leah. She wants to go back into the living room and listen to Jay play guitar, and stroke his cat.

Angeline gets up and stares into the bathroom mirror. She wipes carefully beneath each eye with the pad of her forefinger. "That's cool," she says. It's a new voice she's flicked on, bright as supermarket light. "I'll just tell my stepfather. He punches harder than anyone."

"Don't do that," says Leah. She's seen the bruises on Angeline's arms, purple, like sloppy kisses. "You can't."

"I wake up dead, you'll know it's him," says Angeline. Listless, she opens Jay's medicine cabinet. "What about aspirin?" she says.

"Just don't tell him." Leah wonders what Angeline isn't saying, why a grown man would beat up a girl. Inside her makeup case, the ones and fives ripple and coil, like snakes.

"Why not? He'll see it anyway. You ever sock anyone?" Angeline makes a fist, fastens it to her hip. "You might need to know this," she says, looking at Leah sagely in the cabinet mirror. "You lock your wrist, right? Then you breathe out and *bam*." Her fist doesn't actually sock Leah but it comes close. "My stepfather says go for the gut," says Angeline. "Split your knuckles on someone's teeth."

Her eyes fill with water again. "I'm gonna tell him," she says. "I can't have some crazy baby."

It's true, she might. There's a little sister, Reen, who never says squat. That's according to Angeline. Reen is eleven and she likes to light matches and she likes to watch them burn. She burns trash up on the roof. Reen is how Angeline met the truancy boyfriend, Jack.

Plus, thinks Leah, a person can't just let someone's life fall apart. A person can't let someone get socked in the uterus. And Leah could fix this. She has to fix it. If she saves Angeline then the tube will slide out easy as glass and they can be just regular friends.

"I have some money," she says.

Angeline's attention swivels like a radar dish. Leah can practically hear it ping. She gropes the contents of her pack, unzips the costmetics case. "It's not enough but you could borrow it," she says, and holds it open.

Angeline looks inside. She puts her fingers to her mouth. She stares at Leah, then back at the money.

"How much?" she whispers.

Leah tells her.

"Oh my God. Oh my God. I don't believe this." She looks at Leah with wonder, or horror. "No one ever gives me *anything*."

Loans, thinks Leah. Ever *loans* you anything. She prays this is just a misunderstanding.

"I don't deserve you," says Angeline, slowly. "I don't deserve anyone like you." She takes the case but her gaze stays fixed on Leah. The case is a black patent Mary Quant that took three visits to Bloomies to steal, and Leah is struggling to say she needs it back when Angeline locks both arms tight around her neck and releases a long, shuddering sigh.

Leah waits for disentanglement. When that doesn't happen, she tentatively places one hand between the bone-wings of Angeline's back. It is a narrow, tapering back, with ribs that precisely align with her fingers. Also there is a strap, three hooks wide. Leah's index finger lies across the strap and her mind plays with the hooks while Angeline rocks, a small lapping movement that Leah experiences as sweet, perfect fusion.

"You're so good," says Angeline. "You're such a good

friend." She sniffs wetly. "I would die without you, I swear." Then she steps away. "God, you have no idea," she says, dabbing in the mirror at her eyeliner again. "I thought no one was gonna help me kill this thing."

In the textbook drawings, the womb looks like a Grecian urn, its handles uncurling toward the ovaries.

"Listen," says Leah, because maybe she has one more thing to give. "You're not really killing," she says. "It's just cells in there. They're not even differentiated yet. Not very." She glances at Angeline's midsection. "I mean, they're sort of differentiated," she says, carefully, in case Angeline actually looks at the drawings in their bio text, those delicate sea-creatures curled at the tips. "Like the neural tube? But it's maybe an inch. I wouldn't worry about killing."

This time, when Angeline hugs her, she will touch the quicksilver hair. Not that she is one of those sick sisters.

But Angeline just stares.

"You are fucking amazing," she says, and drops the makeup case into her fringed purse. "You are a piece of work, you know that?"

Fourth period and Angeline will be waiting for her again. All year, since they became best friends, Angeline's been waiting outside bio. She always has urgent, private things to say while the other kids file in.

Then she whispers to Leah during lab.

They're doing fungi—the true, the algal, the sac, the club, and Leah's favorite, the slime molds. But Leah's notes have recent gaps. Her *Rhizopus* drawings have failed to capture the dandelion-grace of the stalklike hyphae of common black bread mold. This is because she keeps looking up from the scope, afraid to ignore Angeline and afraid to whisper back. Yesterday all she said to Angeline was, "Don't forget to copy."

If she goes to bio now she might throw up.

"Let's hear it, honey," says the nurse, her broad hands spread on the metal desk.

It would not do to say she has a tube down her throat. Instead she thinks fast and says she has a spike in her eye.

"Fun, isn't it?" says the nurse. "Welcome to my life. That's a migraine, sweetheart. A pickax headache." She crosses her arms, scanning for damage. Leah concentrates on cranial blood vessels, thinner than rubber bands, tightening. Or maybe dilating—she forgets.

"Ice," she whispers.

"Your mom probably gets them." The nurse rises heavily and pats a vinyl chair until Leah drops into it, one hand cemented to the pretend-offending eye. "Maybe it's your period."

Leah hears the kiss of a fridge opening, the clatter of ice. "I can't miss bio," she says, and starts to cry. Even for fake pain, it's unbelievable, the way it knots the cervical vertebrae, cracks the zygomatic arch. This could be a whole new thing for her, migraine. Robyn Hart, who has shoved her off the balance beam twice, will take one look at her stoic pallor and say, Babe, you need to sit *down*. And Angeline will step respectfully back, breathe her own air for a change. Next time Angeline says, "What're you, kidding?" Leah will sag against the wall, palm to her eye. "Pickax," she will murmur.

When the bell rings she grabs her pack, remembers suddenly to reel from the pain. "I can't miss French," she says, and stands blinking while the nurse scrawls a readmit.

There is a quiz. Baudelaire. Leah, at her locker, moving her lips as if in prayer—*Mon esprit, tu te meus avec agilité*: my soul, you move with ease. Of course that would be someone else's soul. Leah's soul is still lurching around with a migraine and a rubber tube in its throat. Someone taps her on the shoulder, tentatively, twice.

Ice, thinks Leah, God grant me ice. She pastes her hand to her eye, and turns.

It's only Mary Gage, who never talks to anyone in French either.

"I'm dead," says Mary Gage. She is wearing her white rabbit-fur jacket, though it is late May. She always wears it, right through class. "What's with your eye?"

Leah's right shoulder feels heavy from the double tap. Her left feels as if it is floating. She wonders if there is any way to get Mary to tap her left shoulder.

"Nothing," says Leah. "Did you study?"

"Yeah," says Mary. "The wrong poem."

In the moment that blossoms between them, it occurs to Leah that two girls who never talk to anyone in French might have a few other things in common. For example, they both get A's. Also, Leah has her migraines for protection now, and Mary Gage has her rabbit cocoon. Plus maybe, once they've started studying together, Mary Gage would enjoy hearing a few choice facts about balling. *You won't believe where this guy has a mole*, Leah will say.

And now her soul begins to stir. "Répétez," she says, and feels the flapping of tiny, vestigial wings. "Au-dessus des étangs, au-dessus des vallées."

Mary Gage chants.

"Des mon*tagnes*, des *bois*, des *noige*, des *mers*."

Mary Gage chants that too, and Leah is just about to feed her *Beyond the sun, beyond the ether* when she feels her other shoulder, the floating one, tapped hard. It is Angeline Yost, whose mesmerizing existence Leah has almost managed to forget, and Angeline is standing there as if the first bell had not rung, as if the hallway were empty save for dust motes and ghosts.

"Please can you come with me *right now*," says Angeline.

Leah's hand creeps back toward her eye. It gets stuck at her cheekbone. "I can't," she says.

Mary Gage looks panicked. "Par de*là* le sol*eil*, par de*là* les é*thers*," Leah tells her. To Angeline she says, "I'm really sorry. We have a test."

"Oh, God," says Angeline. "Please." She takes Leah's hand in both of hers.

Mary Gage stops chanting. She stares at their faces, then at their hands. Then she takes a very small step back, still staring, and Leah feels a stirring of pride. Angeline Yost, one of the toughest girls in school, is her best friend. When Angeline opens her mouth to sing, quarters drop at her feet. Dollars, even. And there might be an audition. "Please," says Angeline, "it's an emergency, I swear to God." Angeline has a mother who goes for the face and a stepfather who goes for the gut and a little sister who melts down Barbie dolls. Angeline knows where the teeth go during a blow job and Leah believes that even during that particular motion, every feature of Angeline's face adheres to the divine proportion. Angeline Yost is a walking ratio of 1 to 1.618, the golden mean, and even Keats has said it: *beauty is truth.* That is all ye know on earth, Keats said, and all ye need know, and Angeline is practically begging now: "You have to, Leah, I'm goddamn *bleeding.*"

Mary Gage's eyes go wide.

"You," says Angeline, "go. Amscray." She makes *scat* gestures. Mary Gage takes another step back. Leah wants to grab her wrist. She wants to say, save me.

"Mange la merde," says Mary softly, from inside her cloud of fur. Then the second bell rings and she turns and runs.

Angeline can't get her jeans down fast enough. Blooms of crimson spread on her sneakers, on the tiles.

"Don't look at me," says Angeline, but it's her own face she turns away. Her thighs she parts, very slightly, for Leah's inspection. They are smeared, scarlet. "Am I okay?" she demands. "Tell me I'm gonna be okay."

You're the science freak, Leah hears.

A fat shimmering red thread unspools from Angeline's womb and hangs, gelatinous, into the commode. After a few seconds Angeline squeezes her knees together and rocks forward.

"You kind of need to know what's coming out," says Leah.

Angeline peers down, then closes up again. "Just blood," she says. "I think it's still coming."

Leah imagines a teacup, brimming. "You want me to get the nurse?"

"What're you, kidding?" says Angeline. "For a goddamn period?" Leah waits. She can't believe the word needs saying. *Miscarriage.* She stands in the tiny stall with Angeline and listens to her breathe. Finally Angeline looks up. "Look, I need Tampax, okay? I need napkins. I need all the shit you can get."

Leah closes the door gently, digs for a dime, cranks a sanitary napkin from the machine.

"Don't leave me," Angeline calls from the stall, and in the tiled silence of the girls' room her voice has a faint metallic echo.

Leah sucks air through the tube, leans against the Modess machine until the dizziness lifts.

"Did you pass anything?" she finally says. It's a hospital question. A nurse once asked her father that, after whipping the green curtain closed, and Leah imagined her father astral-traveling under his restless white sheet, passing everything, his daughter, his wife, all the scenery of his life flying by.

"No. Yes. I don't know. I'm gonna flush."

"No, *wait*," says Leah. Because now she really wants to know. Because Angeline is Parthenon-beautiful even on the inside, blood tipping from the urn, and Leah wants to know what the body can do. She opens the door without asking and thrusts the napkin at Angeline. "Stand up."

"That is so sick," says Angeline. "Who's gonna look?"

She has no idea, thinks Leah. She really has no idea what is happening here.

"I am," says Leah. "Get up."

Angeline looks at her, surprised. Then she clasps the napkin between her legs, stands, and hops to one side. Leah hesitates. Toilets alarm her. She hates the way they swallow and she hates wondering what they might gargle out. But she kneels, and looks.

Blood forms a macramé against white porcelain. The water swirls densely with red.

She takes a breath, holds it, and dips her hand into the bowl.

"That is disgusting," says Angeline. "I'm gonna flush."

"Don't," says Leah, sharply. The water is shockingly cold. "You could still be pregnant. You have to know." She trawls the red water slowly with her fingers. Angeline leans against the partition, her pale-sky jeans around her ankles, stained, her face still turned away with a grimace, as if to hide a deeper nakedness.

"Is it in there?"

Leah has, in fact, found something. It swims out of her grasp. Slippery fish. She stops stirring and looks. Hanging half-deep in the water is a small, complicated clot, streaming veils of thin tissue. She collects it carefully in her fist.

"If you've got it, I don't want to see," says Angeline.

"You're right," says Leah. "You don't. I have to wash my hands."

She closes the door quietly on Angeline and runs water at the sink, letting it stream through the bowl of her fingers.

"Wait a minute," calls Angeline.

For almost sixty seconds, Leah listens to her silent struggle. She had thought the blood and veiling would rinse clear away, leaving something like the drawings in bio—a glassine bubble, with a tadpole inside. Instead: diaphanous ribbons of tissue, like shreds of Saran, and beneath them something as small and resilient as a lost fingertip.

"It doesn't look like a baby, does it?"

That must be the caul, that ribbony stuff. Who was it born in a caul—Macbeth? No, the other, the one who kills him. Not of woman born. She leaves the water running while she examines the thing she's caught. Tadpole, seems like. Mer-man, head the size of a berry, the face-part blurred. If she squints and thinks hard she sees minuscule arms and maybe these are microscopic hints of hands, just a bit fingery, and he curls around his own bulging belly like a snail.

"Leah, for Chrissake, what *is* it?"

He could fit in her mother's thimble.

"Is it a boy or a girl?"

Those could be eyelids, fused shut beneath the veiling. She decides they are. She imagines them lit by the ghostly blue glow of blood. Everything in this world that he needs to see, he sees.

"Goddamnit, Leah, does it look like a baby or not?" Wailing now.

Leah turns the water off. With a cautious finger she nudges the creature. That maybe could be its penis, that anise seed. Or not. He would have spent his whole life producing sperm, she thinks, whereas Angeline, whose ovaries Leah imagines as two clusters of pearls, was born with every egg complete.

"It's nothing," says Leah. "It's just a clot."

"I don't believe you," says Angeline. "I want to see."

Leah pats the fish dry in paper toweling.

"Maybe I should bury it. You think I should take it to a priest?"

Leah rolls the little fish into a clean piece of paper towel and tucks it into a pocket of her backpack.

"Are you even fucking *there?*"

"Yeah," says Leah. She wonders what would happen if she walked out now. "Listen, I'm sorry. It slid down the drain. It was really slippery. It was just a clot."

The stall door opens with a bang. Angeline leans in the opening.

"Bullshit," she says. Her voice is thick, as if her mouth were packed with blood. Her jeans are up but not zipped. A spray of hair clings to the side of her face. "You're lying," she says. "You saw something." But she is just a girl. "I know you saw something," Angeline says. She is just a strong, unhappy girl with a silvery voice and a makeup case with a hundred and eighteen dollars that she will find a way to keep. Angeline says, "I'll make you tell. You know I can." Leah looks at her. She hoists her backpack and feels the mer-man throb. His heart glows darkly, a small red sun, and she is not afraid.

Breakage

The roofer clicks an orange Life Saver between his teeth, rubs under his jaw. "Tonsils *and* uvula," he says. "Gone." He opens his mouth wide, loops a U in the air with his finger.

"Ouch," says Pansy. She is holding a fragment of Spanish roofing tile. Lately tiles have been sliding off the roof easy as coins, exploding on the patio, scattering orange shards like bougainvillea blossoms. Unwilling to peer in the roofer's mouth, she glances at his neck. Even missing a part, it's enormous. It could pass for a thigh.

"Snored like a man drilling rock," the roofer says. "Wife made me sleep in the den, with the dog."

Pansy sympathizes, because she, too, sleeps in the den, flung face down on the daybed. Robbie takes thirty seconds to fall asleep; he doesn't know where she goes after that.

"How bad is it?" says Pansy.

They are on an asphalt ribbon of roof in Venice, California, examining an eave canted over the bedroom.

Tar paper rasps under the roofer's black shoes. Under Pansy's bare feet it's silent, which is a shame, because the asphalt sets off her geranium toenails—little flares of Maybelline.

Pansy chalks red Xs into the stucco with her shard.

"You got practically a hole over your bed," the roofer says, looking at her sharply.

He knows where the bed is—he climbed out the window. He knows their blankets pool on the floor and stay there. Perhaps he knows that Robbie's magazines are reposing under the mattress, slipping from their slick covers; that the sheets are three-weeks unwashed because Pansy is still waiting for Robbie to remove these accusatory publications, it is a matter of *sheer respect*, and Robbie has not figured this out, does not seem to care, has not noticed that he sleeps alone in linens that are growing rank, like shrouds.

"See under here, paper's rotting. Water gets under the tiles, it runs downhill till it finds a hole. Or makes one." The roofer sinks a thick finger into a gap. "There you are in bed," he says, "thinking all nice and safe, and drip, drip, drip. Then you're fucked."

We're already fucked, Pansy wants to say. She imagines lying in the dark next to her husband of ten months; she hears the breath rattling his uvula like a dry reed. She imagines the word *uvula* rocketing around her mother's brain, triggering fantastical little nerve explosions. "Sounds like plum brandy," her mother might say, looking thoughtful in the disaster site that passed for a kitchen. Or, "That's a Thursday word." How lovely, Pansy thinks, to simply drift above squalor like that. She has not seen her parents in a year.

The roofer is not unattractive. He is one enormous muscle, hairless above the neck, eyes green as traffic lights. "I could do you a new roof," he says. Pansy repeats to herself *I could do you*, thinks of a man drilling rock, and has a fantastical little nerve explosion of her own. "Cost you four thousand bucks," the roofer says.

And it's not even their house, for Chrissake. It's Robbie's mother's house, falling quietly apart one block from the beach, and it's rent-free if they would just pay the taxes and electric and keep the place up, because Robbie's mother has gone to Arizona with her chronic asthma and her chronic boyfriend and her chronic teacup cockapoo.

Pansy puts her face in her palms and inhales through strands of wet hair. Then she spreads her fingers and looks. Down in the yard she sees blond grass gasping for water. She sees concrete cracking in the drive. She sees bromeliads gathering their ugly red strength in plastic pots.

I am going to do something very soon, she thinks. Learn how to garden. Taste some words. Visit my sister. Get on with things.

As she watches through her fingers, a brown-striped cat picks its way around an agave.

"Or we could slap some new tiles on, not like we get much rain," the roofer says. He opens his mouth and shifts the jaw, as if trying to stretch something. "Who ever thinks about a uvula?" he says.

Under Robbie's side of the mattress, women chatter and preen. They pretend to ignore their breasts, which Pansy sees are like baseballs, whereas Pansy's are more like socks with baseballs inside. They deforest themselves with napalm or battery acid, whatever it is women use. Then they and their breasts go jogging. Robbie would worship these women; he would ask how they feel about a thing, he would ask about their day. He would hide his magazines the way she hides her cigarettes.

"House like a marriage," says the roofer. "Got to tend to it. Costs like a sonofabitch, though." He rubs his throat.

Pansy tries it out in her mouth: *tend*. It's a Tuesday word. She wonders if a person, listening in the dark, can hear mold turn to black velvet on the rafters.

"Just slap some tiles on," she says.

Hate

Leah, home from school early, caught her mother in the act—fingers rustling in a Whitman's Sampler, the box all bristly with pleated cups.

"Holy shit," said Leah. She let the door slam. "She *eats*."

Chocolate molecules swirled across the living room, triggered a phantom sweetness on her tongue. She edged toward the chocolate, books still clutched to her chest— trig, physics, nineteenth-century poets.

"I have to gain weight." Helen's voice went gravelly. "Gray says a client complained." She lofted one arm, balletic, and sighted down the length of it. The skin was blue-white, the bones beneath it lucent.

Gray Alistair was the decorator Helen worked for part-time. He had a kindly, shapely beard, which Leah loved. He had coltish French side-chairs, which he absently stroked along their backs. He had a young person named Philip Godchaux living upstairs in his East Sixty-sixth Street townhouse, above the studio. *Houseboy*, Helen said, with the tone she might use to flay an avocado-colored appliance. Sometimes, when Leah visited, the houseboy drifted in and looked at her. He always carried something—a movie magazine, an English cigarette—and his feet were always bare, and golden.

Leah wanted to lick them.

"I thought Gray liked negative space," she said.

"Apparently not on me," said Helen. She plucked a chocolate with meticulous fingers and bit off a corner.

"Stick it in your mouth and chew," said Leah helpfully.

"Don't be wise."

Leah thought briefly about foraging in the box. Her mother always set out normal foods for her—spaghetti, bologna sandwiches, Special K—and kept her company while she ate. Sweets, though, Leah had to sneak. She stole cans of Hershey's, and sipped the syrup in the basement. She stole Sugar Babies, which she chewed in bed.

"Listen." Helen bit off another corner as if it were an aspirin. "Gray's taking me on his next antiquing trip, to France. Ten days." She leaned forward and looked, for a moment, almost dreamy. "You can teach me some phrases," she said, lifting the fine calligraphy of her eyebrows. "Je m'appelle Helen. How much is that fine Louis Quinze bergère?"

"Tell him no," said Leah, frantic. "I have midterms. I can't make up ten days. I'll be doing P.E. the rest of my life."

"No, you won't," said Helen. "You're staying here."

Leah's head began to float, as if helium had seeped between the meninges of her brain. From the ceiling she saw exactly how ten days alone would go. The apartment, without Helen's slight weight as an anchor, would shudder free of the building and drift. The fridge, half-empty, would self-purify until it was as sleek and vacant as the tub. The alarm clock would suffocate in the fold of a sheet, causing her to oversleep and get suspended and drop out of junior year.

She saw herself staring into the bathroom mirror for hours, looking into pores and orifices for the source of the flaw.

"You can handle it, sweetheart," said Helen. "You're sixteen."

"Next month. You can't just *leave*." Leah reached for the Whitman's. Nothing happened. Chocolate seemed to be on the menu now.

"You know, of course, that there's no—that Gray and I would never—" Helen laughed dryly. "He has that house-boy person—"

"Mom, would you *stop?*"

"But if this trip goes well, if he thinks I have an eye, Gray says he'll make me a real decorator, and the houseboy person can answer the damn phone." Helen sat back and, to Leah's amazement, licked chocolate off her fingers.

Leah wondered what would happen if the houseboy said no. She had wandered once into the garden behind the studio, saw Philip stretched out and shirtless, sunning amid Gray's roses. The low waistband of his jeans ignored the hollows of his hips, and when he shifted to look at her, the gaps parted slightly, like mouths.

"I don't know how to cook," Leah whispered.

"Who needs to cook? I'm leaving you fifty dollars and fifty emergency."

Fifty dollars. *Cigarettes.*

"I'll call you," her mother said. "You can't call me in Europe, though. If you need anything, ask the building people. Ask the houseboy. Ask Oleander's mother, if you want."

Entire *cartons* of cigarettes and boxes of Barton's chocolate truffles.

"Oly's getting weird," said Leah. By which she meant that Oleander had a serious boyfriend, an impressively creepy one inherited from her sister, and red needle-spots on the backs of her hands, which Oly wore as if she had been marked.

"Her mother likes you," said Helen. "God help me if we're in some old inn with the toilet down the hall."

Fifty dollars a week, she could buy Coca-Cola and Oreos and Trix, like at other people's houses. She could buy coffee rings from Cake Masters, and actual Tampax, instead of pads. With the fifty emergency she could buy a dragonfly pendant with a tiny spoon at the bottom, like some of the girls had. To wear—with a silver chain, just to wear.

"You can eat breakfast at the greasy spoon and dinner at the Chinese," her mother said. "Just make sure the silverware is clean. If it isn't clean, sweetie, ask for new."

Everything she bought would go on a list. *Things to Hide Before She Gets Back.*

"You can go to the movies," her mother said. "Just make sure it's an afternoon show and you don't sit near any men. At least four rows away, Leah. You have to count."

Leah began counting. Number of days with windows open to the airshaft, so smoke could sift out. Number of three-year-old codeine tablets in the medicine cabinet, remnants from her father's sickness. Inches of vodka in the cabinet over the fridge, ditto. How many kids she knew, and whether that was enough to have a party, and whether the party would be boring because she had nothing to barter for their company except old codeine and vodka, and she might be too scared to tell about those.

"Can I wear your fox jacket?"

Who knew, she might do anything. She might meet a boy in the park. He might push her up against a tree, abrading the silver fur.

"They eat all that butter and cheese, don't they," her mother said. "If I come back fat, just shoot me." Her glance flicked toward Leah's thighs, an involuntary inspection that Leah always seemed to pass but that somehow made her feel stripped.

Helen put the cornerless heart of chocolate in her mouth and closed her eyes. "Not to school, how's that," she said. "And not in the rain. I can't afford a new one." Her ribs rose and fell; they glowed through the silk of her blouse.

Leah waited.

"At least I've found my calling," said Helen. "I can make anything beautiful."

Friday morning, Helen pressed her hand to her daughter's face.

"Mom, I'll be fine," said Leah.

But Helen kept her hand there as if she hoped it might leave a mark. "Shayna maideleh," she said. "Grandma Rose called you that." Then she lifted her leather suitcase.

Leah went to school and came home and froze, listening hard to nothing. The image of a large bed containing her mother and the slightly corpulent Gray floated into her thoughts, causing intense disturbances.

She sank a mop into a pail of hot water, added one cup of white vinegar, and washed her floor.

While the floor dried, she ate the first box of Barton's truffles entire and drank a quart of milk, an excess that made her want to race crazily down Broadway, dodging cabs. Instead she prayed her one prayer in the bathroom until the Barton's came up. She poured bleach into the toilet and Windexed the mirror and looked in the medicine cabinet. Then she poured lemon oil onto a chamois and rubbed the teak dining table. She tried to rub the Breuer chairs, but they were varnished so it didn't take.

She turned on every lamp and light switch. Thought, *I could sleep anywhere.* Helen's white sofabed: a sacrilege. Or tent the table with a sheet and sleep under it like a child. No, she might get grabbed—bony feet sticking out like handles.

She did forty-four trigonometric equations, solving for X. She loved X, loved the way it swung from each equation like a gymnast off the unevens, landing squarely on the page. After math Leah graduated the items in the medicine cabinet by size and arranged them for equidistance. She brushed her hair one hundred strokes.

Then she poured approximately three teaspoons of vodka into a glass, lit a Winston and stalked about in her nightgown smoking and drinking like a divorced lady, except not really drinking, just touching the tip of her tongue to the vodka.

The apartment, to her amazement, stayed tethered to the building.

"Get this," she told Oleander on the phone. "She's gone."

"How long?"

Oly was allowed to do anything she wanted but had no privacy to do it in. She and her mother had to share a big bed, which stayed unmade. Clothing sprawled on the floor and people flopped on the sofa without considering sneaker placement, and books were left face down with their spines stretched open, and sometimes Mrs. Prideau would dogear a hardcover book or write in it, and you could take a beer without asking even if you were fifteen, but there were no coasters.

Anywhere. That's what Mrs. Prideau said. Just set it down anywhere.

Leah thought about damage control, about what Oly might dismantle given a solid week. "Just till Sunday," she said.

"I call the living room," Oly said. "Guess what Nestor's got."

Nestor was nineteen. He never considered sneaker placement, and he tended to wander around a room picking things up, things that had been carefully sited or maybe even graduated by size, and putting them down haphazardly, as if browsing for a souvenir.

"You can't sleep here with a boy," Leah said. "My mother would burst a blood vessel."

She padded around in socks. She took inventory of various relics: silverplate frame with photograph of her dad, whom she was not supposed to dwell upon; the doctor said it would keep a child from Getting On With Life. Right. Lacy waist-high underwear, folded in thirds, best not to look. Two cream silk blouses, ironed on low and hung with tissue paper in their sleeves.

Listen, Helen had said, *it makes everything sound new.*

Her father's wedding band, broad and faceted, folded into a Kleenex.

Touching everything exactly once. She had to do that. When she was done touching everything once she tried on her dad's wedding ring. It slipped off every finger but the thumb, and then she couldn't tug it off.

Lights blazing, she prepared for sleep—turndown of top sheet by 45 degrees, followed by calibration of self into the exact mathematical center of the bed.

"She's probably got a lover," said Oleander. "She's probably in some hotel."

What Nestor had was a tank of nitrous from Mt. Sinai, where he was an orderly. The tank was tall as a fire hydrant—dark green, with a rounded bottom so it couldn't stand. "I bring back the empties," said Nestor, gripping it with his knees. "And air ain't stealing, right, baby?"

He screwed on the regulator, turned a knob. The tank sighed once. Oleander, lying on the sofa, lifted her head from his lap to watch. It wasn't fair, thought Leah, the way their bodies touched and untouched without consequence, the way his arm brushed her collarbone and then moved away without a rupture.

"My mother is in France for work," said Leah, "and nitrous *oxide* is not *air*."

She wondered what would happen if she told them to leave. They would say no. They would say: What are you, crazy? Then she would be wearing the loser hat, and everyone would stay exactly where they were, but quiet, and ugly. What was it Nestor's profile reminded her of? Mole? Something that burrowed.

"Nitrous oxide is a gas," she said, curling her toes into the white shag rug. "N–two-oh."

"Anything you say, Doc." Nestor palmed the plastic mask and fitted it to Oly's face. She closed her eyes to receive it. He kept his hand there, holding it over her nose and mouth.

"Where's the strap?" said Leah.

"France doesn't sound like work to me," Oly said into the mask, muffled, and went into a spasm of giggling.

"Don't want no strap," said Nestor. "You pass out, you better hope that mask falls off."

Oly laughed. It sounded like underwater. Then her laugh trailed off like the end of a melody. When it started again it rose to a slight hysteria, with notes of keening. After a while she lapsed, distracted, into quiet.

Nestor didn't seem to notice anything different. "Kill people with a strap," he said.

"My dentist uses a strap."

"Dentist got you plugged into two tanks. One for oxygen." He had the bright, black eyes of an animal, too. Anteater, maybe. Something with a snout.

Oleander mumbled a word into the mask. It sounded like *daddy*. Her facial muscles slackened. Her arm slid off the sofa, striking a beer bottle and hanging at an odd, languid angle.

"Jesus," said Leah, lunging to right the bottle. A rivulet of beer streamed under the sofa and Oly's fingers trailed in the liquid.

"Just beer," said Nestor amiably, and closed his own eyes, preparation for the sacrament of the mask. His hair, dark and shiny and long, fanned out across Helen's white bouclé upholstery. If there had not been a spillage crisis Leah would have wanted to stroke it, bury her face in it, see if it smelled of fur.

"If it gets on the rug it is not *just beer*." Leah yanked Kleenex from a box. She wondered if she was now officially engaged in partying, an act that might require vigilant cleanup, but that would overnight license her to use language like *wasted* and *trashed*. She wondered if Oly and Nestor would do anything on the sofabed, later, and whether they would leave some kind of stain.

"Listen, Doc."

Nestor's chest rose, shuddered slightly, and fell. His breathing under the mask was even and deep. His lips widened into a private smile, and after a while his knees parted, letting the tank tip forward on its rounded bottom. The tank struck Helen's faux-Giacometti coffee table, bit a chip from the glass top, and shot out a wandering, thread-like crack.

Bloodless, unseen, the crack slivered under Leah's nails. It laddered up her spine, spidered into the sinus below her left eye. Then it bored slowly into bone—one of Helen's migraines, maybe. Shrapnel from something Leah had not known could explode.

"I am so dead." The words tuneless as breath.

Nestor let the mask drop and held up a long, silencing finger. His eyes remained closed, his head tipped back. His smile did not narrow for a long time. After some minutes he opened his eyes and said, "Re-entry," and slowly leaned forward. He pulled the tank back and inspected the damage.

Then he looked at Leah, who had all ten fingers deep in her hair, lifting it from the roots.

"Stop that," he said. "Listen. I am the Dark Lord of the North, Servant of the Three Pure Ones. He with his right foot upon the tortoise and the snake. And I am telling you this one truth, Doc. It is *just fuckin' beer*."

Leah stared at him.

"The Tao of Nitrous," he said. He stretched his arm out toward her and then his hand, as if offering a scrap to a small animal. In his palm, face down, lay the mask. "Come here."

He didn't even offer to pay.

"Where do you get glass?" said Leah.

"From sand," said Nestor. "You get glass from sand. Come here. William James did this shit, you know."

Did what? Broke tables? There had to be a place that sold glass. Maybe a window company. She crawled toward him. His eyes were again closed. She sank her face into his palm. She didn't know who William James was. They didn't have a television—she didn't know who a lot of people were.

"Say it," he said. "It's just beer."

She breathed in, like at the dentist. After a few breaths her brain blinked on—a pinball machine when the quarter drops in.

"Say it."

Two quarters. Pinball lights began flashing. Flippers sprang to attention. The machine lifted off the ground and began to spin. Steel balls floated like blue planets.

"Say it, Doc."

Her mother was going to kill her. She laughed right into Nestor's hand. Her mother might have a lover and there might be a stain and her mother was going to kill her. Nestor's hand was a cup she wanted to float in and he was going to let her. Electrons swirled and sank in her body. Her private area felt joyously shocked, as if lightning had struck nearby.

"Say it."

He was making her feel things and he hadn't even moved.

From Oleander came a low symphony of consciousness—the sounds of long muscles being stretched, the sucking of beer off fingertips. A noise like purring.

Go back to sleep, thought Leah.

She buried her face in the hand of the Dark Lord of the North, and drank.

Sunday evening, she snagged a window seat on the Seventy-ninth Street crosstown, watched rain crawl sideways on the glass. Felt the bus shake as it plunged into the transverse.

Philip answered Gray's door barechested, despite the chill. Leah looked at his feet: ambery, as if he'd had them gilded. And bony, with long, golden toes.

"It's the child," said Philip. He slipped into Gray's older-gentleman voice as if into a cloak, and in that moment Leah understood that Philip knew Gray in some intensely private way, but that he did not love Gray.

"Exceedingly wet child," said Philip. "You can come in if you don't drip."

Dripping, Leah hesitated, searching for something clever to say. Philip glanced past her, up and down the dark sidewalk. The street was isolated. "I'm locked out." She fingered the housekey in her pocket. "The super's not home and I think my mom keeps an emergency—"

"Yeah, yeah, yeah."

Philip opened the door wider. The sweep of his arm struck her as both courtly and sardonic. She stepped into the hall, its walls papered with antique maps that yellowed elegantly under varnish. The fur of Helen's jacket had clumped into wet, sleek needles. When Philip led her into the studio she saw tidepools of shadow beneath his scapulae. She knew what an invert was: a man with carnal appetites for another man. But she couldn't imagine what Philip and Gray might actually do beyond the lighting of English cigarettes, the caressing of French sideboards.

"I'm ruining your rug." Her hightops—perversely red, to annoy her mother—were dark with rain.

"Not rug, darling. Aubusson. And not mine." He poured from a decanter, faceted, like the ring on Leah's thumb. "I just vacuum it."

He handed her a bulging glass. Leah swallowed and burned. She swallowed three more times and felt something tip between her ears, and wondered if that was the alcohol or the half-tablet of expired codeine or both.

"I partied so hard last night," Leah said. She thought this sounded fairly impressive, so she kept going. "I was just totalled," she said. "I was just wrecked."

"You forgot snockered," said Philip. "And shitfaced. Were you shitfaced?" He ran the back of his hand down the front of her jacket. Then he sniffed his fingers.

"What?" said Leah, alarmed.

He stepped toward her. They were exactly the same height. She did not want to meet his eyes up close but she also did not want to look down and see his nipples, which were tiny and brown, with infinitesimal bumps. Instead she backed up to the edge of her mother's shiny desk and sat on it. Under the shine was an old Victorian table with paws, but Gray had talked an auto-body shop into spraying it black.

On the table was a real tortoiseshell tea caddy for Helen's private miscellany, which might or might not include an actual housekey.

"Rain," said Philip, "is the second most sensual liquid. Would you like to know the first?"

"No," said Leah. She cleared her throat.

"Your loss. Taste." He ran a forefinger down the spiky fur again and held it near her mouth.

"Philip," said Leah, ducking her head, "I'm *locked out.*"
It sounded good. She almost believed it.

"Taste," said Philip, and moved in so near he was standing between her knees, and it was almost unbearable—the beauty of his chest, the splendor of it, hairless, lean, the way it gave off its own light, and how that light reminded Leah of a lamp with a peach-colored scarf tossed over it.

Her hands felt like heavy appendages, large as stop signs.

She could twist away now and fumble through the tea caddy and leave, key or no, because she had learned what she came to find out. Or she could open her lips and admit the shocking tip of the finger of Gray Alistair's houseboy, tasting first the clear water, the cool non-taste of it, and under that—in the channels of his whorled fingerprint—notes of salt, of Remy and Dunhill, of whole-grain leather, of the inside of a pocket. Of oily, fat black crumbs nestled in foil. Of smells from other people's bodies.

She could taste all that. And then she could take her enormous hands, her freezing palms whose creases were improbably filling with sweat, and press them to the source of light directly in the center of Philip's chest.

"Jesus Christ," she said, remembering what else she needed to know. "Where do I get a big piece of glass?"

Philip tipped his head, so his gaze slid down the top of his cheekbone.

"From me," he said. "I order it. What size?"

"You order it?" said Leah. "That's it? You just pick up the phone and *order* it?" She closed her eyes. "Coffee-table size," she said. Nestor was right. She had thought he was wrong but he was telling the truth. It was just beer.

And as it sank in about the glass and the beer, a second fragment of the Tao of Nitrous was revealed unto her: that now would be a fruitful time to keep her eyes closed.

Philip's gold fingers skated onto her hips. He buried his face under the wet fur and bit her on the shoulder. She did not jump.

"Keep your shirt on," Philip said into her hair.

Leah did not know if he was being literal or snide. She stood perfectly still. He slid his hands under the rabbit jacket to her ribcage. None of it counted, because Philip was neither entirely normal nor entirely boy. She thought how the space he encircled was *cage* as much as *rib*, air more than bone. She thought how this might be a reason, empty and pure, that a person might not eat.

"Control yourself," Philip muttered.

When he kissed her, he used everything: lips, teeth, tongue, hair, the sides of his face, both hands. He did this until Leah started feeling like the sand inside an hourglass.

Then he took a sudden step back. "Just curious," he said.

How do I love him, Leah thought: let me count the ways. He emitteth his own light; he controlleth the elements.

Also, she loved the way he could simultaneously want and discard her. She even loved knowing that if she lunged for the tea caddy, he would grab it away and look for himself.

Did it casually, then. Pulled it toward her as if bored, as if she had fingered its contents a dozen times. And there was, in fact, a key, though definitely not to her apartment. "Voila," she said, and held it up brightly.

"You got what you came for," said Philip. "Maybe you should go."

"Right," she said. She reached out and touched the arch of Philip's eyebrow. He blinked. Then she put her finger in his ear. The ear was serpentine like the inside of a shell, and faintly sandy. A sound came out of her. Tiny, animal-istic. One syllable.

Philip grinned.

"Wanna fuck?"

She hit him.

She didn't know where the command came from—*hit him, in the face, hard, now*—only that she was sure she was supposed to do it. Was astonished to find that it burned the hand, astonished again when her left cheekbone det-onated, when she discovered that a slap, if one is at the receiving end, feels exactly like the word: *fuck*.

"Sorry," said Philip, "but you don't get to do that."

Do not get to slap, she thought. Do not get the soft and whispery first kiss. Do not get the boy's ring to wear on a thin gold chain.

"Invert," said Leah.

But this was not what she wanted to say. What she wanted to say was she was sorry.

The glow from Philip's chest deepened to apricot. His fingers flexed. "Get out."

"You get out," said Leah. "It's not your house. It's not even your rug."

He grabbed the silvery fur. Helen's jacket made a tiny

tearing sound. "I hate you," he said. He took a fistful of orange hair, pulled her head closer. Whatever was going to happen would happen now.

"Bitch," he said.

She was not afraid. She loved how the thing that was wrong with Philip, the piece that was jagged or missing in him, seemed to mirror a piece that was missing in her.

He searched her face as if the room had gone dark.

"I hate you," said Philip, only lower, a murmuring, and she felt a closing, which was her eyelids, and then an unfolding, which was something entirely else, something sweeter even than the sanctuary she had found in the hand of the Dark Lord. Philip gripped her arm, and here is where he made the sound of a moving current, here is where he pressed his mouth against hers so that she thought of the palms of saints or was it pilgrims, here is where he said *hate you* into her mouth and she said *I hate you too*.

Excelsior

Osiris, god of the dead, keeper of keys, daytime manager of the Excelsior Hotel for Women, waded into the elevator ahead of Helen, then led her down a dim green corridor. Opera floated from a phonograph. It grew louder as they walked. Seaweed carpet, walls the color of algae—Helen felt water rising.

"This is a good thing, a corner room," said Osiris, and stopped at the blind end of the hall.

The phonograph was clearly her neighbor's. Helen spotted a pinch of silver, like chewing-gum foil, jutting from the woman's lock. She picked it out discreetly, and felt instantly better.

"Most private," Osiris was saying. "You look like a person in need of privacy."

It was a question. Helen ignored it. She knew why he asked: he had spotted the signs of a woman from better circumstances—blue velvet headband, hair glinting from a hundred strokes a night. Osiris shrugged with his eyebrows, pushed the door. Then he stepped back, letting her enter first. Helen understood: If a person was going to rent a room, she had to believe from the start that it was hers.

"The corner rooms have private toilets," Osiris said from the doorway. "It is a nice feature."

She recognized the room as if from a dream. Windows bristling with bent Venetians, hers. Blue rug blistered with coppery burns, hers. Scrim of grime over landlord-white walls, all hers.

Helen opened the bathroom door with one finger, took a quick inventory. Toilet, sink, a ceramic toothbrush holder mortared to the wall. She would have to buy Comet, bleach, a pair of rubber gloves.

"The shower is down the hall."

Also a bathmat, washcloth, and a plastic basin—to stand in, if she wanted to bathe here, like Venus on that shell.

"It's perfect," she said. "How much?"

"Madame," said Osiris, "it is not perfect. Forty-five dollars a week, payable in advance."

"A few pictures on the wall," said Helen, "long white curtains, a little desk ..."

Osiris unshelved himself from the doorframe. His skin was the color of caramel, and gleamed down the middle of his scalp. "No removal of the fixtures," he said. "No addition of fixtures. No nails."

"Oh, you won't see holes." Helen tugged at a bureau drawer. It balked. She'd paint the dresser some startling twilight hue, slick a bar of Ivory over the glides. "And I'll leave the curtains. You'll like it."

"No nails," said Osiris. "No screws, no glue, no tape, no

paint, no alterations of any kind. No cooking in the rooms. No men past the lobby. No visitors in the rooms after nine p.m."

Helen tried to read the manager's face. She could not believe he meant all these things. Men, naturally. But tape?

Next door someone lifted the phonograph needle, replayed several keening notes. Fat ladies, she thought. Cats in heat. At home she couldn't think straight if Leah's stereo was on—but Leah had just moved to Amherst taking all her stereo components, dangerous with dials, and those records with asynchronous names. Airplane, Jefferson. Floyd, Pink.

"You forgot no loitering," Helen said lightly. "I saw the sign. Is there a lease?"

"No." Osiris dangled the key from its wire ring. "Each week, there is a receipt."

The room asked of her precisely nothing. It did not demand that she track down the perfect Oushak carpet, though this was a thing she could do. It did not require twelve brilliant centerpieces, like the ones her employer, Gray Alistair, let her design for a client—lavender roses spiked with pheasant feathers, bristling from asparagus vases. ("Clever girl," said Gray, "the quotidian and the sublime.")

No, this room craved only the smallest embellishments. She had only to nail up a dozen yards of voile at the windows, which stared vacantly into other buildings. She had only to paint the dresser—deep violet, yes, with new cut-glass knobs. She had only to marshal daisies into a water glass.

"You won't see nail holes," said Helen, turning so earnestly to Osiris that she actually touched his shirtsleeve. "I promise," she said. "I won't even be here that long. I just want to fix up the room."

"Fix?" Osiris's palm swallowed the key, yet it seemed to Helen that far beneath his calm surface rippled some private amusement. "Something needs to be fixed?"

The opera voice sank an octave, hung low in the air. Helen wanted to shut the door, but then she and the manager would be closed in. It would be inappropriate.

A pay phone was mounted on the wall by the elevators. When Osiris left, Helen fished a dime from her wallet, used it to call in sick. Then she visited the common bathroom, just to see.

Two young women, one Puerto Rican maybe, were on their knees, washing dishes and saucepans in the tub. The tub looked greasy, collared in gray, and there was no scouring powder, no sign that the women intended to scrub it, after.

The women looked up at her with curbstone eyes. Helen nodded and backed out, her fingers seeking the key in her pocket. Far down the hall, something flashed on the carpet outside her door. It winked as she walked. Tin foil—a gleaming mystery-strip of it, laid down in her brief absence like a welcome mat. As she approached, it sucked fluorescence from the ceiling, shot it toward her in dull flares.

In the garment district that afternoon Helen bought a half-bolt of sheer white voile, dollar a yard, and maneuvered it bodily into a cab.

She bought twenty pounds of glass gems from a crafts shop, all blues and greens. She bought a dozen bags of baby white shells, a glue gun, and a hundred waxy sticks of glue. She bought a five-foot ladder and a reversing drill that could twirl screws out as well as in.

The taxi waited, ferried her elsewhere, waited. She bought robin's-egg blue paint, a roller, an extension stick. The taxi waited.

Osiris, stationed at his wood-grain desk in the lobby, planted his palms on the arms of his chair and half rose. Every gate has its guard, thought Helen.

"How can you work there?" she said gaily. "You have no light." She hauled her first load of purchases to a vinyl armchair, dropping only one bag along the way. "You need a lamp," she said, trying not to pant. "One of those handsome banker's lamps, the brass ones."

Osiris stared at her. When Helen returned from her second trip to the cab, grappling with the ladder and the paint, he was peering inside the fallen bag.

"None of these things are for here," she said. "Don't worry. They're for my job."

"Your job," he said, and it was hard to tell if he was blocking her way or merely stopping her for a chat. "What kind of job for a woman requires a drill?"

"Dressmaking." Helen propped the ladder against a wall. She, too, could have a private amusement. "You'd be surprised." She was not used to perspiring, else she would carry a handkerchief.

"No running a business from the rooms," said Osiris.

She resisted the urge to wipe her face with her sleeve. She resisted the urge to clasp Osiris by his sloping polyester shoulders and beg. He examined the glue gun and shot her a question with eyes the color of jade.

"One moment." Helen attended to her purse, came up with a twenty. Osiris studied his nails, which were shapely and clean. It was too clearly a bribe, Helen realized. "Please help me carry the fabric," she said. "And maybe the ladder. If you would."

For services rendered, apparently, Osiris would take a twenty. He hoisted the bolt of voile, gripped the ladder, stooped for two gallons of paint, and lumbered into the elevator. White threads streamed out behind him in the hall. Helen's neighbor was back at it, her phonograph leaking high, tremulous notes from under her door.

Not like alleycats at all, thought Helen, startled. More it was the sound of an icicle growing, drop by inching, gilded drop.

Opening the door, she saw the razor blade instantly. Another mystery gift, it lay on the threshold, edge pointed in toward the room. For one dissociated moment she thought a high note had snapped off from the song and taken this shining form, a lethal slip of steel.

Helen planted the sole of her shoe on the blade and slid it out of Osiris's view.

"After you," she said.

She stood trembling until Osiris, his back turned, steadied the bolt against her dresser, encircling it with broad hands. Then she picked up the razor and dropped it into one of her bags.

Osiris lifted the loose end of the fabric and extended it, wavery as a veil.

"I look forward to this dress." He gazed through the fabric at Helen's ankles.

Helen sharpened her voice. "That's *one layer*," she said, and set her parcels on the bed. The razor burned in the bag like an ember.

Still peering through the voile, Osiris lifted his attention to the hem of Helen's skirt, which precisely bissected her kneecaps. Then he raised his gaze.

"Your hand," he said calmly. "It is bleeding."

A red line, seeping.

"Occupational hazard," said Helen musically, closing her fist. She sensed that it might not take much—a deep cut, a sentence of any gravity—to end this little *pas de deux* with the manager of the Excelsior Hotel for Women and bring down the full force of his rules.

"Please, could you help me?" She opened the ladder by a window. It would hardly do to climb in a skirt. "The blinds are broken," she said patiently.

Osiris, who had again cemented himself to the door-frame, held up his left hand and waggled the ring finger; like hers, it was banded in gold. "You have a home," he said. "You have a husband."

"I do," said Helen, "and I don't. He died four years ago. Otherwise I am sure he would be here. Taking down the blinds," she said pointedly.

"I doubt that," said Osiris mildly. "No men permitted beyond the lobby."

Helen, recognizing this as humor, smiled slightly.

"As if." It was a thing she had heard her daughter say.

Osiris ignored the open ladder. "You know what this place is?"

"Yes."

"Not a hotel," said Osiris. "S.R.O. You know what this means?"

"Yes."

"Single room occupancy," said Osiris. "You understand this?"

"Yes."

"It means welfare," said Osiris. "Some of these people, they drink without a glass. You meet your neighbors, you will know what I am talking about. Have you met your neighbors?"

"Yes." In the bathroom the women had turned to examine her. They exchanged a word, and then one woman made a grating sound that might have been a laugh, though water was sluicing loudly into the tub, so perhaps Helen had been hearing things.

She allowed Osiris to study her from the doorway. He seemed to be on the verge of something.

"Mrs. Levinson, what is it exactly you are trying to fix?"

She patted the ladder. "Right now?" she said softly. "Just the blinds."

Osiris crossed the room, climbed. The man had bulk and yet grace, too, as if inside him stood a younger man, agile and lean. He unlatched the blinds, bending back to avoid the blossoming dust. Bound the blinds in their cord and handed them down, gingerly. Dust blanketed Helen's wrists.

She sneezed twice, tucking her head toward her shoulder, birdlike.

"May God bless you," he said. "The blinds will come from your deposit. The trash is down the hall and to your left."

Leaving her room, she stepped into an outpouring of song. She had not been attending to the music, but now, moving toward the source of it, she ran into the shard of a high note, and froze. The note trembled in the air. Then, like a piece of crystal, it burst.

Helen walked slowly down the hall, embracing the broken blinds. The voice folded its wings and began to drop, as if a woman, weighed down by sorrow, was sliding slowly to the floor.

She knew the things she could not fix.

For example, she could not fix the cataract that dulled the floorboards. Could not fix moldings that met without marrying. Could not scour away the poultice of grease that had baked beneath the radiator.

But a room always held something you couldn't fix. Her mother's slashed curtains, bleeding sunlight through the cuts: she remembered that, and cotton festering in a mattress gash. Five years old, transfixed in her parents' bedroom by a snowstorm of feathers that flew from pillow wounds.

You want to shit on our marriage? Lena's fingers still white around the knife. *I'll show you shit. I'll show you shit.*

The feathers weighed less than the atmosphere they

rode; when Helen closed her fingers around the downy stuff and then opened her hand to peek, it was empty.

She changed into a pair of new, stiff Wranglers. She painted the ceiling robin's-egg blue, using the roller with its extension pole and newspaper to catch the drips. She sanded the rough spots and painted the walls camellia-white, tinged with pink. This took three mornings. The razor lay brazenly on a windowsill, gathering its powers.

Each day at noon, she locked her room and followed the carpet toward the elevator, headed for a half-day at work. Coming and going, she heard behind her the near-silent breath of her neighbor's opening door.

And each day Osiris dropped by around ten, watched her from the threshold.

"You never sleep here," he said, and waited.

He tried again. "When you leave, your deposit . . . "

He left her door ajar, always. He was all propriety.

"Do you always make the ceiling blue?" he finally asked.

"It's how the Victorians painted porch ceilings," said Helen. "I just brought it indoors. You forget how small a room is if you're thinking of sky."

He leaned in the doorframe with the ease of a man in a reclining chair. "It is beautiful, the paint," said Osiris. "The paint can stay."

Five mornings at the Excelsior and she had barely put food in her stomach. She was losing weight again, approaching that ecstatic emptiness.

One afternoon, Gray Alistair came up behind her and slipped his hands clinically around her waist, as if taking her measure for a dress. His appraisal was strictly aesthetic;

he had that houseboy person upstairs, Philip. "You look like one of those Holocaust people, darling," said Gray. "You look like one of those Jews."

She wanted to tell Gray: My *mother* was one of those Holocaust people. She wanted to say: I *am* one of those Jews. But it was not a thing Gray would want to hear.

Instead, she went to Sloan's and bought jumbo bags of M&Ms. At first she consumed them in the following manner: Place M&M vitamin-style on back of tongue. Fill toothbrush glass with water. Swallow. Repeat. But soon she began to suck on them slowly. Soon she began to chew.

It would not do to fall in love with sugar. It would not do to fall in love at all.

"Who is that woman?"

The song was a bowed head. Helen could not tell if the grief lay in the notes or in the silences between. It seemed to her that something was missing, perhaps an answering cello, but maybe silence was an instrument too—she knew nothing about music.

"Not welfare," said Osiris. "Not one of the drinkers. Who knows who she is? Who knows who anyone is?"

"I wish she'd play a happier record."

"What record?" said Osiris. "She is singing Gorecki."

Helen, stitching chain weights into a curtain hem, stopped moving her needle. Gorecki she didn't know. But singing? She stared at Osiris.

"What did you think? She is crazy," he said. "She will tangle with you, if you let her."

"Tangle?"

She moved the curtain off her lap, slipped past Osiris, and stepped outside. One of the young women—the one who had laughed at her—sat on the carpet by the singing door, hugging her knees. Her feet were bare, lustrous and long. Her skirt was a riot of green leaves, and her eyes, when she opened them, were wet. Helen looked at her in astonishment. It seemed to her that the walls of the corridor were slowly streaming with water.

Osiris coughed. Preface to an edict, Helen was sure. No sitting on the carpet; no public displays of music appreciation.

"Don't," said Helen, without turning around, in a voice that came straight from the razor on her sill. "Just don't." She placed her palm on the singer's door. She thought she might feel its molecules trickling, loosened by song. Instead, only metal, cool and hard.

The woman rose. Her long feet rolled heel to toe on the carpet as she walked.

Fragrance of saffron. Curry. Green peas buttoned into long-grain rice. Helen was used to drawing nourishment from elaborate, imagined meals; she was not surprised, then, to find herself communing through a closed door with Osiris's gift of lunch.

He did not knock. "Mrs. Levinson?"

The lunch beamed images to Helen through the door— of a small, unrenovated kitchen in one of the boroughs, Queens, it must be Queens, where a handsome if thickening woman, a woman of, oh, forty-seven, who still draped herself in black before visiting her mother-in-law, tasted something from a wooden spoon.

Helen scrutinized the point of contact between glue gun and glass jewel as if cauterizing a nerve. When she thought she looked fully absorbed she called, "It's unlocked."

The door, coaxed by the toe of a black shoe, sailed open. "My wife has sent you a meal," said Osiris. On the bureau he set a Pyrex bowl with a taut Saran skin. Then he held up a small square of tin foil, waggled it to catch the light.

"Also," he said, pleasure expanding in his voice, "you have a letter."

My God, thought Helen, this man laughs without laughing. Maybe he knows how to talk without talking.

This man, she thought, would be a delight to live with.

"Your wife," she said. He was a good man—of course there was a wife. The tin-foil letter she decided to ignore for now; if it contained another razor, Osiris might have to act.

The bowl pulsed with onion and cumin. She wanted to inhale this food. She wanted to attack it with an enormous fork. No: she would dispose of it quickly, bloodlessly, odorlessly. Getting rid of food had been the major preoccupation of her childhood.

"My wife," said Osiris, "cooks for sixteen families." He seemed to be saying something entirely else, something encoded. Helen was sure of this. *My heart runs wild*, something like that. She noticed, too, that he lingered at her bureau this time, rather than returning to his post at the open door. "She makes deliveries in our car," Osiris said. *You remind me of a moth, with dark eyes on powdery wings.* "It was no trouble to make one portion more. I hope you like."

Helen liked and she did not like. The plate of food made certain demands. It could not be disposed of down the hall. She would have to buy Baggies to smuggle it out so the smell would not escape. The thought of being caught made her dizzy. She gripped the plastic gun. A filament of glue settled on her wrist, a fine, stray hair. A child's hair. She was forty-three years old but she might have been twelve, looking at a plate that she refused two mornings ago and that now appeared, relentless and sodden, at every meal.

Food is life, Lena would say, and Helen, wilting under the smell of curry, suddenly grasped that it was the mechanical quality of that voice, not the rescuscitated food, that made her gag.

"You don't take nourishment," said Osiris. "Aren't you hungry?"

Was she hungry? She never knew.

"Open your letter," said Osiris.

Helen put down the jewels and the glue gun, made appreciative sniffs toward the Pyrex bowl, and patted the foil envelope. No razor, thankfully, just a nugget of some kind. Turning her back to Osiris, she opened the shiny triangulated flaps. Inside, a slip of paper, folded into a wad. Even smoothed out it was hard to read, the pencil smudged.

STOP SENDING YOUR EVIL THOUGHTS UNDER MY DOOR. STOP SENDING YOUR DOG WITH THE BLACK TONGUE INTO MY ROOM.

No wonder the razor, Helen thought.

"May I?" Osiris extended his hand.

Helen shook her head. It seemed to her that the singing woman had taken off the top of her skull and revealed a dark, seething mass of brain. This seemed strangely beautiful. Listen, she wanted to write back, that razor was over the top. It sharpens itself, just sitting there. Listen, she wanted to write, there is no damn dog.

She held the note respectfully by the edges. It reminded her of a story, and she wanted to remember what it felt like, capturing and holding a man's attention with a story.

"Do you know how John Lennon met Yoko Ono?" she asked.

"A Beatle?" he said. "I should care?"

She told him anyway, exactly as Leah had told it. An artist, Leah had said, and for this one show, Yoko dragged a tall ladder into the gallery. "John Lennon showed up," said Helen, "and he looked at everyone's pictures, and then he came to Yoko's ladder."

Helen stopped. In a mortifying coincidence, she too had a ladder. It stood open before a window, where she had nailed up a long flourish of voile.

"He climbed, of course," said Osiris. They both looked at her ladder. A jet of flame shot through Helen's face.

"At the top," she said—because what could she do but finish?—"was a little card glued to the ceiling. On the card was one word: *yes*. That was the moment John Lennon thought, this is the woman I want to marry."

She waited for Osiris to ask the same question she had asked Leah—what if the card had said *no*? But Osiris did not say anything. Instead he nodded, not only with his head but davening slowly from the waist, as if recognizing something deeply internal yet far away.

"What else could he think?" Osiris said.

Helen could think of nowhere to escape but up. She picked up the glue gun and the penciled note, tucked an open bag of glass jewels into the waistband of her jeans, and climbed.

"What are you doing?"

"You might not want to watch this part."

"And why is that?" Osiris smiled at her. Really, he had the oddest sense of humor.

"The ceiling is a fixture," said Helen. "No alteration of fixtures." She smiled back at him. It was a lovely thing, to make a small joke, and when was the last time she had smiled at a man? Next door the crazy lady sang *husband*, she sang *gone*, she sang *never*, she sang *dead*.

"Really, Osiris," said Helen, and his name in her mouth was a spiral, ascendant and long, "go look at the view."

The ladder trembled and she froze on the topmost rung. It bore a metal placard reading DO NOT STAND ON TOP STEP. She ignored it, seeking balance. Don't flail, Gray had told her. Balance comes from within. A stillness of blood, an awareness of breath, how workmen stay safe on ladders, darling.

Helen squeezed hot glue around the edges of the note.

It was only seven steps from the bureau to the south window, but Osiris's status shifted with the trip: from landlord to guest. From distant observer to—something closer. Gentleman friend. He appeared to be listening to the orchestra of traffic, eight stories down.

"Tell me now," he said, "why you are here."

Helen pressed the note to the ceiling. She dug a glass gem from the bag.

"A compulsion, maybe," she said lightly. "You really can't let go of it, can you."

"And why should I let go of it?" *And why should I let go of you?*

A jeweled border began to glitter around the note.

Osiris said, "You remind me of my daughter, with her dollhouse."

The razor glinted at Helen from the sill.

"My daughter made chairs out of Dixie cups," said Osiris. He kept his back turned. How courtly, this small gift of privacy. "My wife gave her earrings from the five and dime, and she made chandeliers. What do you do that is any different?"

"Nothing." Helen clicked glass jewels in her palm. She didn't look down.

Her secret room had left New York. Sometime in the past week it had floated south over rooftops until the room was just water and sky. In her new coral bedspread, Helen imagined the sand; in the violet bureau she saw tropical dusk.

She leaned down toward the windowsill. Stretched to reach it. Tweezed up the razor with wary fingertips.

She had just touched the gun to the razor's spine when she felt herself moving toward light, toward a membrane of voile and filtered sun. The ladder rocked, righted, rocked again. She heard the long, searing bite of a blade through drapery, and she was vaguely aware that her hair was sailing.

When Helen landed she had a new arrangement of limbs, unconsidered and regretful, like a broken clock.

Osiris held his fingertips to her carotid artery. Helen felt it leap. She heard the sound of her name. He moved her fingers to her mouth and nose. She exhaled upon them. He rose, perhaps to call for help, when Helen stopped pretending to be unconscious and said, "Osiris. Don't go."

He squatted again. "Does anything feel broken?"

Helen thought about this. Her legs appeared to be floating, her lower spine burned, and she had absolutely no desire to move. "My elbow hurts," she said, almost happily.

Osiris palpated the joint as if testing a plum. "I think not," he said. "May I call you Helen?"

"Yes." She decided to continue floating for the immediate future. The room was adrift with feathers. It was peaceful and still, and no one expected her to fix a thing.

"I can tell you what she thinks," said Helen suddenly. "She thinks I slide my evil thoughts under her door. She thinks I have a dog with a black tongue."

"Not in my hotel," said Osiris, causing Helen to fall in love for the second time in her life. "The black-tongued dogs, they are the ones who can't be tamed." And he was doing it again, talking in code, so that his thoughts travelled like the light from stars. *My heart cannot be tamed.* "The black tongue, it tells you the granddaddy was a jackal," he said. "Such a dog will love only one master."

Somewhere in Helen's body a telephone began to ring.

Osiris pressed her hand to his face. He held it there a long time. Then he stood. When he returned he held the fragrant Pyrex bowl.

She would lie awhile on the scarred blue rug. She would eat from a spoon. She would watch the feathers rise and fall. Her room was unfinished but she was done. Any time now, she would answer the phone.

Delacroix

So many things Leah wants to know about men, and here she is, alone with her investigations in an actual man's room, ears radaring for footsteps, face buried in Terrence's shirt. She sniffs. Hangers clink. Shirt releases a tang of fresh air and Clorox. Or maybe she imagines the fresh air: she knows Terrence grew up on a farm.

Terrence's khakis hang neat as a folded flag. The hanger sags, that's the kind of closet it lives in, but Terrence has folded his pants with deliberation, tending the crease.

There are rules to snooping in an actual man's room, and Leah is surprised to find that she knows them. One, no looking under the mattress. Two, no reading anything not brazenly on display. Three, no uncrumpling of waste-basket matter. And four, no rushing to judgment. No deciding, for instance, that a man who wears poly-cotton shirts, who wears *short-sleeve* poly-cotton shirts, is carrying the loser gene. Her father, for example, wore only long-sleeve shirts—shirts with elegant, curving collar tips, the cotton fragrant with starch. She saved them all. Six years later she still wears them to bed. She would have saved his jackets but her mother sent them to the Goodwill.

Terrence's room is a laboratory; she's just scanning the data. She's allowed to check whether a man's toothbrush bristles are straight or splayed (they are splayed), if he uses a comb or a brush (comb), whether that comb is tortoise-shell or black plastic (black plastic), and if a man lets the hairs collect in its teeth (he doesn't). Does he drop them in the wastebasket or on the floor? The rules are clear on this: no searching for hairs. But she can open one drawer if she doesn't rummage. For the first time she sees the word *Jockey* stitched into broad elastic. For the first time she sees that a man folds his underwear. This makes her feel deeply, gratefully relieved.

Hands in her pockets so she won't rifle, she evaluates the yellow pads rising in stalagmites around Terrence's Smith-Corona and the books bristling with scraps of paper. Ulysses. Mrs. Dalloway. One she's never heard of, called Night. Like her, Terrence is just renting a frat room for the summer. Every morning he takes a book to the kitchen and pours corn flakes and milk into a white plastic bowl; the flakes get soggy while he reads. Then he takes two yellow pads to the Columbia library and works on his dissertation, leaving her alone and bored in a narrow building of locked doors.

"In the twenty-four-hour novel," he has typed, each black letter runneled deep into onionskin, "the constricted framework of a single day may yield the deepest exploration of the human condition—"

Leah can't help it: one hand flutters free and strokes the page, reading the keystruck letters like Braille. She's a bio major, she can't tell if he's saying anything new, but she knows exactly what he means. It's like examining a single epthelial cell and seeing within it the human body, the entire living universe. She wants to bolt down the metal-edged stairs of Alpha Epsilon Pi and tell Terrence this: that they are kin, she and him, that they see through the same lens, that he should love her with all of his heart.

But he'd know she was looking. Boy steps out of a cornfield, he probably trusts her not to look.

By the end of freshman year Leah was sick of trees, allergic to sky. She missed New York so bad she could eat concrete. For twenty-five dollars a week, so cheap she barely had to work, she booked a summer room in a Columbia frat on West 113th. Minus the frat boys: they'd deserted. They're rich, she figured, it must be clean. She hauled two chestnut-leather suitcases on a bus down from Amherst, then onto the IRT; by the time she rang at the brownstone her shoulder muscles were bronze knots.

Silence, then staircase clopping. *Male* staircase clopping, dropping in pitch as it neared. A young man opened the door and rubbed one eye with his knuckle, unseating his glasses. "Hi," he said. He looked a little rueful. "I'm Terrence."

Other tenant. Grad student. Awaiting her arrival; had her key. Leah smiled the one-sided smile she had practiced all year in her dorm room, a smile that said *hey, big boy,* on the left side where it went up. On the right side it said *don't get chatty in the hallway, don't wander around in boxers, don't get any ideas.* She wanted a sorority but they didn't rent.

He took one suitcase, said, "I hope you like quiet."

"I adore quiet," said Leah, a little too loudly. Her voice echoed in the tiled vestibule. She liked that he was holding her suitcase. She liked the way his body looked, strong, but spare.

"Good," he said, "because it's just us."

I'm in a French movie, thought Leah, with subtitles and train stations, lovers padlocked into stares.

"Where am I?" she asked.

Terrence searched her face as if trying to put a name to the green of her eyes—a watery tint that Leah called algae. "Oh," he said suddenly, "second floor front. You're lucky. I'm on the fourth." He wore black jeans with a white t-shirt that said nothing, not even on the back, as she saw when she followed him in. This seemed promising. Guy in a blank t-shirt was not likely to get too intense, was not going to play Led Zeppelin at the top of his stereo's lungs. She followed him past a living room with an old leather couch and up a staircase with a low creak.

Her door was soiled with stickers. Sports helmets, the Playboy bunny. Someone had smacked the stickers on with absolutely no respect for symmetry, which made her fingernails itch.

"La clay," said Terrence, and handed her a key. Clay. *La clé.* As in French.

"La plume de ma tante," said Leah—all she remembered from Mademoiselle Répétez. She liked Terrence's laugh: deep, one syllable. She wanted a black coffee with four sugars, a shower, and a cigarette, in exact reverse order. Then she wanted to iron her clothes, if these cretins had an iron on the premises. Then she wanted a date-nut bread with cream cheese from Chock full o'Nuts, like she grew up on. She froze the key in the lock until Terrence took an accommodating step back. Then she opened the door. Then she slammed it. It banged back open.

"Mine had a petrified sandwich on the desk," said Terrence, amiably. "Penicillin factory. What've you got?"

"Bug," said Leah. Her tongue thick. *Roach* was not a word she wanted in her mouth, never mind the unspeakable plural. "Oh, God," she said, pulling at the skin on her arms. A thing that crawled might wander up a sleeping body, antennae oscillating. It might scale the ridge of an ear. Leah wanted pumice, she wanted Brillo. She felt her skin bubble as if something garnet-dark had already slipped beneath it.

"I don't see it." Terrence peered into her room. "You want me to kill it?"

"Them."

"You want me to kill them?"

She wondered if roaches could trickle through zippers, if there was any place they could not go.

"I need another room." Skin still rippling.

"They're all locked," said Terrence. "But we could bomb it." She looked at him. "Bug bomb. Gas 'em out," he said cheerfully. "It worked in my room. You could sleep there." Added, as if it scarcely needed saying: "I'd take the couch."

"You would? Really? Jesus," said Leah. His expression flickered. "That's really nice of you," she said, trying to atone for the *Jesus*. "Thank you. Thanks a lot." She had never slept in an actual man's bed. His pillowcase probably smelled good. "You're not from New York," she said.

"No one's *from* New York," he said. "I came up in Kansas."

Leah saw metal pails in a dawn-dark barn; she saw swallows in rafters; she saw Terrence assisting with the feeding of pigs. She saw him doing what needed doing without complaint, because that's how a boy would grow up, out there. Wherever Kansas was.

"I'm from New York," said Leah.

He set her suitcase down next to the wall, as if suitcases should not be dropped just anywhere, and glanced at her. He seemed to be taking her measure again and finding her taller, or perhaps tougher, than she first appeared. You don't understand, she wanted to say, we're not all tough in New York, some of us were afraid of everything, the glissade of silverfish in the bathroom, the spurts of waterbugs, fat and oily, in the basement, the men in the park with their hands at their flies. Terrence looked at her and his face was open like a plain—not that Leah had ever seen a plain, but in his eyes she saw wheat standing slender and strong. Even his spectacles were wide-eyed, as if he'd passed some time searching horizons.

"Did you grow up with wheat?"

"Wheat, corn, sugar beets," he said. "It was a small farm. My parents live in town now."

"Sugar beets." It sounded reassuring. She liked sugar. It was one of her staples, along with coffee, coffee yogurt, and cigarettes. "How long does a bug bomb take?"

"Twenty-four hours," said Terrence. "Couple days to air out. We could set two, if you like. We could set four. Whatever you want."

"I want four," said Leah. "Are you sure about the couch? Because I could—" But she couldn't. Her mother lived in L.A. now. She had nowhere else to go.

Leah walks. She's partial to 109th, where years ago they found a head in the trash. A clean, bloodless cut, as Leah imagines it, lipstick smeared, bruises gone from aubergine to green around the cheekbones.

She walks to 82nd and Fifth and sits on the broad steps of the Met and smokes, then goes inside and broods over the mummies, dark-boned in their luminous wrappings. Better the damp dissolving pine, she thinks, better the holes drilled in the base of the box. Here is what survives: seven shirts, pale blue and white, with elegant collar tips. Here is what survives: the tang of Sea Breeze, locked for a lifetime in a daughter's olfactory lobe.

That night at the frat she hears typing behind the closed kitchen door; she smells the chemical sweetness of the bombs. Next day she walks more than a hundred blocks to Greenwich Village, chewing Aspergum all the way for her racehorse ankles. While she walks she pretends Terrence is her narrow-legged boyfriend, that he leaves her languishing for his love. In one scenario he strokes her face and says her eyes are like emeralds. Then he refuses to notice her, which exquisitely primes her for more languishing. It is a perfect imagined relationship, really. She has never pined for a man before. She rather likes it.

Terrence, passing her on the stairs at Alpha Epsilon Pi, obliges by not getting chatty in the kitchen, not wandering around in boxers, not getting any ideas.

"I aired your room out," he says a few mornings later, looking up from a bowl of drowned corn flakes. "Swept the little guys up. It should be okay."

"You're amazing," says Leah. She smiles at him with half her mouth. "I'm in your debt."

"Maybe I'll collect," says Terrence.

At the temp agency she takes a test, clocks in at 92 words per minute. She wonders if typing is her one skill, her truest destiny. She gives them the phone number at the frat, but the boys must have locked up their answering machine, and she is rarely there to answer.

"May I ask you a strange question?"

Leah looks up from her strawberry chocolate shake, straw flattening in her mouth. She has been ordering the strawberry chocolate at Three Guys since she was, oh, five. Pinball counter in her brain starts racking up points. He said *may* I. *Ping*. He's still standing, didn't slide into her booth. *Ping*. He has that innocent, worried face, as if he's been scanning the sky for crows, clouds, whatever they worry about on farms.

Also, he did not say personal question. He said strange question. Much more intriguing. *Ping.*

In Leah's fantasy-life, girls have been calling the frat at all hours, then hanging up when she answers. She pretends that Terrence has stopped coming home at night; in the mornings he shows up in clothes disheveled from unfamiliar beds. A liquid pool of suffering, entirely self-created, has opened up just below her solar plexus.

"Ask away," says Leah. This sounds so polished she almost regrets it.

"Ah," says Terrence. It's a beginning. His fingers make rapid diagonal crawls through his hair until several chunks stick up. His cheeks are flushed but his eyes behind the wire-rims are dark and clear. "I don't quite know how to say this," he says. Leah subtracts one *ping.* "Would you come to Paris with me?"

They have had exactly four nonimaginary conversations up to this point. Two were about bugs. One was coffee. She can't remember the fourth. And now, in her blue vinyl booth at Three Guys, a door swings open inside her whole self. It practically bangs open. It hangs shuddering on its hinges.

A door, where she had thought there was a wall.

"You're not going to scream or anything," he says, and takes one small step backward, palms up, placating.

She could be anyone.

"Yes," she says happily.

"Oh, don't scream," he says. "You just look so—interesting. I've been wanting to go to Paris, and you seem like a person who—and there you were, reading."

This is true. Leah is reading *The Lives of the Cell* by Lewis

Thomas, specifically the part about organelles. Most of this stuff they covered in bio, but Leah never gets tired of cells.

"I mean yes I will go to Paris," she says, and inside her the door swings into a big grin of a doorway. Then it sails clear off its frame.

He is the only person she will ever meet who says *gosh*. He says it now, sliding into the booth.

Leah had no idea that boyfriends just presented themselves like that. She wonders exactly who he thinks he is inviting, the real Leah or this other creature, Restaurant Leah, the one who says Ask Away, the one who says yes. It is not a word she is used to saying.

"I don't have any money," she says. "I mean, I have about three hundred dollars but it has to last till school."

Terrence corrals the tabletop accoutrements and slides them into a row. "Well, you could buy us a dinner." He glides the salt forward a few inches. "Would that be okay? And you could do the reading." He moves the pepper. "I could suggest some biographies, that sort of thing. You could walk us through the Louvre."

"That's *it?*" says Leah. She doesn't mean it the way it sounds, though. Jesus. Her face heats up.

"Not exactly." Terrence gives her a long look of pure concentration and it is almost unbearable, as if he had just laced his fingers through hers. Finally he moves the jam. "But there are other reasons I asked you."

"Really." Restaurant Leah coils a strand of red hair around her finger, exactly like a woman who gets invited to Paris periodically and has learned to consider each offer on its own merits.

"You seem smart," says Terrence. Forgetting, she smiles at him with her whole mouth. The jam-packet holder must be the knight, the way it moves up and over. *Check*, she wants to say. *Mate.* "And you don't seem clingy," he says. "Gosh, I can't believe I'm talking like this."

So these are conditions he's setting out. Leah likes conditions. She likes knowing where things stand. She likes that he chose her over all those other girls.

"I wouldn't cling if you paid me."

"I wouldn't pay you," says Terrence. His nose seems to have straightened a little; he looks eighteen now, easy. "Say, do you play chess?"

If you frequent cafes, you will at some point encounter a Turkish toilet, a "squatting" affair that may be little more than a hole in the floor.

This from Fodor's. Leah is having trouble enough with the airplane, which is little more than a few tons of steel falling through a hole in the sky. She does not need toilet trouble on top of this. The success with which the airplane stays out of the ocean stands in direct correlation with her grip on the left armrest, which at some point she needs to release to visit the lavatory. Unfortunately she failed to consider this when Terrence offered her the window. Now his legs are a turnstile between her and the aisle. An aisle passenger might just be getting up to stretch, but everyone knows what the window passenger is getting up to do.

"How's it coming?"

He nods at the book that has dropped to her lap. He's

taken over the history reading, all those Louis-by-the-numbers. Leah knows the French kings only by the legs of their eponymous chairs: the florid, the fluted, the curvaceous with carved shells, absorbed by osmosis from her mother, the decorator. Terrence is doing the history because Leah mistrusts libraries and never went, despite the list he slipped under her door. The prudish crinkle of plastic covers, due-back cards spattered with dates—they make her anxious. Only thing she likes is the official library card with its embossed metal plate. Even better she likes her new passport. She likes being the kind of woman for whom a passport is an absolute necessity. The way men just ask her to Paris and all. When she gets back to Amherst she will fling it onto her desk and leave her door open; maybe someone will wander in. This guy took me to Paris, she will say. We'd just met, I swear to God. He paid for everything.

Plus how was she supposed to fit all those books in her suitcase?

"Listen to this," says Terrence. He's reading *Next to God: French Kings and their Courts*, a library book, he'll have to schlep it back. "When Louis Quatorze went strolling around Versailles, his gardeners ran ahead and hid behind the fountains. When he approached one, they turned it on. When he passed, they turned it off. Then they'd get the next one going. All those gardeners sneaking around." His face is lit with expectation.

"Why?"

"No water pressure." He sounds triumphant. "But guess how many fountains."

"Twenty. Fifty."

"Fourteen hundred," says Terrence. "The king thought they all sprayed at once."

"Poor gardeners," says Leah. And while she's at it, poor Terrence, thinking he has brought Restaurant Leah, and maybe even Negligee Leah, to Paris.

Terrence yawns hugely behind his hand. "What are we doing tomorrow?"

Leah grips the guidebook, her place lost. She's been skipping around. She ignored the hotel part because Terrence took care of that; he has booked a moderate hotel, six nights, in St.-Germain-des-Prés. She has yet to correlate the neighborhood with its arrondissement number. She has yet to study the map. She tries to remember through her fingers the little she's read.

"I thought the sewers," she says. "You can climb down into an actual—"

"Next," says Terrence. He seems amused.

"It's a real museum," says Leah. "I mean it's clean. You can't fall in or anything. It has historical displays."

"Of sewage," says Terrence.

"Yes. No," says Leah. "A sewage *system*." Streams and tributaries, she wants to tell him, rumbling black rivers, snaking pipes. She wants to follow its tunnels; she wants to see the murky, beating heart of it. She wants to find out if she is attracted or repelled, or maybe both. "It wouldn't be in Fodor's if it wasn't clean," she says.

Terrence's seat is reclined. He raises it slightly to look at her. "We have a week," he says gently. "I've been saving for three years to have that week."

She has done something ungenerous, something bad. She chips a flake of polish off her thumb, polish she applied yesterday, clumsily, with Maybelline. She was fairly sure the woman Terrence invited to Paris would have hot red nails, like flares.

"I'm sorry," she says. "Let's start with the Eiffel Tower." Terrence waits. "Or the Louvre," she says.

"Ah." His eyes close and he turns his face up to the air vent. "Picasso. Cezanne." His eyelids are slightly blue. "I want to see every room in the Louvre," and he falls asleep with his rosy lips parted, like a child's.

We are going to do things, Leah thinks. *There is going to be a bed.*

A sheet of light slides under the windowshade. She flips to *Museums*, reads just enough to learn that no Picassos or Cezannes hang in the Louvre. They're in the other, the Musée d'Orsay. She wonders if Terrence's last thought before sleep was that already she has let him down.

Badly. She plays chess badly.

A horn, half muted, honks in the airshaft of the Hotel Geneviève. Leah investigates, finds treillage nailed up on the airshaft wall, and a French pigeon on the opposite sill. "Why does it honk?" she asks Terrence when he emerges from the bathroom, his face damp. "Is it the bird or the acoustics?"

"It's the accent," says Terrence. He smiles at her from across the room, which puts him about seven feet away. She has never seen a smaller bedroom. Or a bigger bed. It's only a double, but it sprawls almost to the walls, pulsing with purpose, flashing bedlike messages.

She wonders if Terrence has noticed. "Let's go find a café," she says.

"We just got here." He rattles through the wardrobe for hangers.

The bed starts humming from the force of its gravitational pull. Leah feigns deep absorption in her suitcase contents. She is fairly sure that the hum is coursing down Terrence's bones, tugging blood to the epicenter. She digs for her hairbrush. "Excuse me," she says, and squeezes past.

That's where he does it, in the little bathroom. Comes up behind her so that the brush freezes near her ear, and locks his arms around her. He is stronger than she would have guessed. That part feels nice. He exhales with his whole body and she takes a shuddering breath with hers. The brush drops to the vicinity of her hip. He rubs a nipple through the leotard and in the mirror they both watch him rub it. The lower half of Leah's body opens like a flower, and much to her interest it is a flower with ruffled petals, that petticoat flower. Peony. Then he fits a hand over each breast.

Leah knows, has always known, that a person's molecules can fly apart like an exploding galaxy and disappear. It doesn't take much.

"Kiss me," says Terrence.

The kiss he gives her is a movie kiss, all folding and enfolding, followed by attentions paid to the earlobe with teeth and tongue as if it were a Life Saver. Then he backs her up to the bed, murmurs into her hair, and reads straight from the boyfriend script.

"You are so beautiful," he says, "and I am so lucky."

Leah stares at the lamp, which is shaded with a pretty Provençale fabric, while Terrence takes the time to do certain things.

"I'm scared," she says, when she has finished studying the lampshade. Her mother would find it busy—yellow, with spiky green leaves arrayed between red blossoms.

"Why?"

She makes a small evasive maneuver, turns her face away.

"Is it me?" says Terrence. "Do I have a smell?" He laughs, but the hand stops moving; he appears to be taking stock, studying her in lamplight. When he speaks again his voice is low with new concern. "You're not a virgin, are you?"

Things she fears: a fissure, a rift, the streaming loss of Leah molecules.

She nods against his shoulder. Not that it's true. Not technically. Though Philip disliked girls, so maybe it didn't count. Maybe all five times didn't count, considering he went back to roaming the park at night. She was not afraid, those times, because Philip was both attracted and repelled; he wanted nothing from her but the satisfaction of his curiosity.

"Gosh," says Terrence, up on one elbow. "I didn't know they made them anymore." He takes her chin and turns her face toward him. His irises are the color of walnut shell, with burnt flecks. "You've brought a present into the bed."

The hand resumes its slow spidering. Moving with new

deference, it tips a sweetness into her arteries. It is only following an ancient genetic course. It is only doing what
people do.

"Not a present," says Leah, struggling to sit up.

In answer, he dips his fingers directly into her blood-
stream. Red corpuscles flow over and around the fingertips,
bumping and rolling.

"But you like it," he says.

"I'm not ready." The petticoat flower waving its petals
like an undersea plant. "I thought I was ready, but I'm not."

Her clothes are still on at 5 a.m. when she wakes to a
tang in the bladder. Terrence appears to be dead, his mouth
fallen open like a cup. He took a sleeping pill, for jet lag.
Leah, who believes that cells are little circadian clocks
with ticking protoplasm, did not.

She confronts the toilet with some anxiety, anticipating
the maelstrom flush. Runs water in the sink so Terrence
won't hear her pee, then stands respectfully back before
pressing the button. At least it isn't a Turkish drain. And
what if she makes an odor in the bathroom, and then Terrence goes in? She tightens her muscles like a lid on a jar,
presents herself to the mirror.

Terrence's mistress sleeps only in mascara and rumpled
sheets; she wakes with a libertine stretch. Leah, on the
other hand, has packed a flannel nightgown with
rosettes. She has forgotten mascara; her lashes are nearly
invisible. It seems entirely possible that the more Terrence insists on breathing her air, the more translucent
her face will become.

He brought the wrong person, Leah thinks.

＆

It's so generous, how even a sixteenth-century building—darkened lobby, no elevator—gives every tenant the gift of a balcony. Sometimes a Juliet balcony; often, a slice of mid-air Paris deep enough for geraniums and a chair.

She tells this to Terrance over chess in a café—a café, mercifully, with a normal toilet. Leah checked before she ordered.

"You need to think ahead," says Terrence. "Get your queen into play." He takes her knight. Terrence travels with a magnetic set, a vinyl mat that never totally lies flat. His brain seems to require frequent engagement: with chessmen the size of thimbles, with the books that cram his suitcase. *Listen to this*, he keeps saying, and Leah inclines her head to indicate listening.

Her own brain requires engagement with concrete, cigarettes, caffeine, and codeine for her ankles. Codeine is legal in Paris, only they call it *Prontalgine*. Her brain does not require a trip to the Louvre this afternoon, never mind the multiple trips Terrence envisions. Leah imagines a towering directional sign in the museum lobby, a sign depicting wings and halls and studded with arrows and Roman numerals and the names of artists, and she feels herself sinking.

"Could you order me another café crème?" she asks Terrence. "I'll be right back."

"Pas de problème." He smiles at her. They are okay this morning, now that he grasps and even seems to admire her virginity. She doubts he will admire it more than two nights, total. That gives her tonight. She limps down narrow, unwashed stairs, opens the germ-infested door to *Dames* with two fastidious fingers. After, she washes up in cold water—there is no hot, there is not even any *soap*—for sixty seconds. God knows what the waiters do. They touch the plates is what they do. Walking delivery systems, evolutionary marvels, conveying French penile bacteria to the American intestinal tract.

So much for ordering actual food.

Leah studies her ghostly eyelashes in the mirror, then gathers her hair into a sloppy chignon. If I were French, she thinks, tucking in the ends, sex would just be sex. It would be like eating. It would be like taking a drink of water.

The buildings are so beautiful, she thinks, every balcony a gift, and I am so deficient.

An ankle, the right, releases a squirt of neurotransmitter. Leah hobbles to the bottom stair where she sits, massages the damage and eats a Prontalgine, her third. Is Terrence checking his watch? Are bodily functions even now crossing his mind? There was a line, she will say, I had to wait. I felt faint, she will say. I just sat on the stairs for a few.

Maybe if she lies quite still on the bed, and and makes herself disappear.

She threads her way back to the table. Her chair, she is startled to see, is occupied. Two pawns and a bishop now lie on Leah's side. Sitting in Leah's place, playing her game, is a woman with—with balconies. There is no other way to say it. Her skin is the color of *café crème*. Her hair looks like mocha fluff.

I have not been paying attention, Leah thinks.

"Je vous en prie," says the woman, and half rises. *I pray you.*

"No, no, no," says Terrence, and pulls over a third chair. "You're winning," he tells Leah, and gives her that farmboy smile. In the presence of this other woman she notices suddenly how white his teeth are, how desirable. Like eggs. "This is Marie-Ange," he says. "Marie-Ange, Leah."

Twice. He said it twice. Marie-Ange, Marie-Ange. The name gleams like lacquer, taffeta, topaz, gold.

"It's Leah Sofia," she says slowly, "if you really want to get French about it."

"Allo," says Marie-Ange. She offers a hand with immaculate nails, unpolished, the crescents at the tips as white as moon. "It is okay I am playing?"

The French stir their coffees so slowly. They sip. The little cup is an hourglass. It is supposed to run its course. Leah disposes of her *café crème* in four swallows. Marie-Ange seems not to have noticed hers. Did Terrence order it? Will he pay? Really, her hair is like the froth on steamed milk.

"Go ahead," says Leah. "You're killing him."

Marie-Ange resettles a tiny knight, forcing Terrence to choose between pawns. "So," she says. "Two Americans in Paris. I hope you are enjoying?" Her voice a glass bell. "I lived in New York for two years. Terrence—" she says it *Terrance*—"says you are born there. Very exotic. Like your hair." She smiles at Leah.

"My hair," says Leah, "let's talk about *your* hair."

"Leah," says Terrence, but she can't help it, her hand dipping into the confection that floats around Marie-

Ange's head. She might as well grasp at vapor. Silk, in the gaseous state.

"Where did you live in New York?"

"By the Central Park. But I was very small." Leah waits for specifics but Marie-Ange is drinking water, she is realigning her pawns, she is lighting a French cigarette from a blue package.

"Marie-Ange used to work in the Louvre," says Terrence. "She's offered to take us around."

"Today?" says Leah. Was she really in the bathroom that long? Jealousy shifts and bubbles in her ribcage; it stretches out rubbery arms, invitation to a dance. Her jealousy is neither male nor female; it is more of an imp. She wonders who conjured it, Terrence or Marie-Ange. Maybe Marie-Ange's hair, though she doubts it.

"Terr*ance* says you have not yet been," says Marie-Ange.

"Jeez," says Leah, "all I did was go to the ladies' room."

"The Turkish drain," says Terrence.

"Not this one," says Leah, sharply. She is enjoying herself in the darkened ballroom behind her sternum. She is dancing the ugly dance. It makes her feel alive. Nothing in Paris so far has made her feel this alive.

Terrence and Marie-Ange glance at each other across the chess mat. A span of understanding forms between them. Thirty-seven bridges across the Seine, thinks Leah: it is one of the few things she remembers from the guide.

"The Turkish toilette, it is not so bad." Marie-Ange nudges some of the cloud out of her face. "You know, if I show you the Louvre, you won't have to read all those books."

"Oh, my God," says Leah. "Did he tell you my sign,

too?" Where is it coming from, this gumcrack laugh? She was wrong: the signs in the Louvre are not her enemy. The signs in the Louvre are nothing.

"Leah wants to see the catacombs," says Terrence. "She wants to see the sewers."

"And why not?" says Marie-Ange. "You can judge a city by the sophistication of its sewers. It's in your books, I'm sure. Your girlfriend has been reading after all, Terrence."

Leaning toward him, she is even more balconied than Leah had realized, more pillowy of hip. Leah eyes the apple of flesh on her upper arm, the way it promises to taste of caramel.

Her jealousy whirls her. It whispers: Terrance, Terrance, in time with the movements of their waltz.

The museum stretches low and long for blocks. For Leah it's just a sprawling gift shop: postcards waiting to be plucked, pretty bookmarks she can share with her sophomore roommate.

"After the Sorbonne," Marie-Ange is saying as they approach the ticket booth. "All my friends were so—how do you say? Jay-loss?"

Leah is chewing a Prontalgine for her ankles, which still hurt, and practicing her Attentive Gaze, one she might assume before each major work of art. The Attentive Gaze stops short of *stricken*, which might seem narcissistic; rather it is a shock of concentration in the face of great and complex beauty.

"I was a guide," Marie-Ange tells Terrence. "A docent,

yes? Can you imagine, every day I inhale these paintings. It was a dream." She grasps Leah's elbow. "You are too quiet," she says, shaking her arm. "I proclaim your punishment. You must choose. What do you like to see first?"

"Terrence should pick," says Leah. "I'm bad at museums." She makes no move to reclaim her arm; she likes this little moment of belonging, like an errant child, to Marie-Ange.

"No one's bad at museums," says Terrence.

"I'm lousy at museums."

"Don't make it difficult," he says. "You just look. You just feel."

"Oui," says Marie-Ange, "what is it you say? There will be a quiz? There is no quiz, Leah Sofia."

Somewhere in her skimming, she must have seen a name.

"Eugène Delacroix," she says.

Terrence opens his wallet and pays for all three tickets before Leah remembers that the Louvre was to be her treat.

With no apparent museum-guilt, Marie-Ange walks them past saints and warriors, past horses flashing hooves. She steers them through long galleries chilled by marble, Leah occasionally walking backward to peer at a radiant Christ.

"Here," says Marie-Ange finally, gripping both their wrists to make them stop. "She is the one I love."

The girl in the painting is laid out in death, wearing white, for purity. A priest stands at her head, and a young man embraces her knees in grief.

Entombment of Atala, the label reads. Terrence opens his mouth. Shuts it.

"You know this work?"

"The name," he says. "Atala."

"Yes! What else you know?" Marie-Ange has the Attentive Gaze down pat. Her lips are parted, as if a lover has grasped her by the shoulders, and her fingers curl at her sides. Leah follows the line of one voluptuous arm; the skin has prickled.

"She's from a book," says Terrence. "A novel. Early eighteen-something."

Leah is impressed. She has never read anything that would help her in a museum.

"A book," says Marie-Ange. "You are a good docent, Terrance. She is too young to die, yes? She has died because of her self. How do you say?"

"We say suicide," says Leah. "Don't you? *Suicide*."

Marie-Ange gnaws momentarily on a cuticle, then seems to remember herself. "Okay, she has died of suicide," she announces, "because she wanted to be of the church, a nun. This guy, he is an Indian, he want to be her husband. And so she drink the poison. Instead of the marriage bed. She do not like to be carnal." The accent, in her excitement, seems to thicken. "Is not yet of the Romantic period," says Marie-Ange, "but is so romantic, yes?"

Leah thinks about Atala's hymen, intact beneath the cloying shroud. She decides that Atala would hate being grasped about the knees. The painting starts working through her occipital lobe like a lesion.

"That's a little extreme, suicide," she says. "Just to avoid being carnal." She looks at Terrence. Maybe she looks at him a bit too sharply. Maybe Terrence returns the look with a movement about his mouth that might be ironic, or sympathetic, or something entirely else.

Without unlocking her gaze from Atala, Marie-Ange seems to be tuning in. Leah can feel it: the change of frequency.

"I mean," she says, not knowing what words will come to her next, or even why, knowing only that she is to be the force of damage on this day. "I mean, sex or death," she says. "It doesn't seem like a hard choice."

Marie-Ange turns the Attentive Gaze on Leah, then on Terrence.

"No?" he says. "Maybe she was afraid."

"That's pretty afraid," says Leah. "That's pretty ridiculously afraid." Then she clamps her lips together. It's a pretty painting; it deserves better. Agitated, she steps away from Atala, causing the right ankle to misfire, causing her to dig for another Prontalgine.

"Yeah, well," says Terrence, and his voice is not unsympathetic. "Maybe that's how some girls feel."

The moment seems to teeter violently on a fine point that Leah cannot quite locate. If she could locate it, she would walk widely around it and straight out of the Louvre.

Marie-Ange claps her hands together. They are dimpled, and the noise is soft. "Well!" Her eyes are about fifty watts brighter. She swivels her attention back to Leah, arches a high, thin brow clearly in thrall to the tweezer, and says in a voice that could have been scraped off the concrete of New York: "Moving right along!"

Terrence has already moved right along. He is several

paintings ahead, studying a round canvas crammed with nudes. If Leah had gardeners they'd be running ahead, switching the pictures around. She turns slowly and focuses on Marie-Ange, luxuriating in the heartbeat of a pause.

"Moving right along?" She watches the Bunsen burner flare in Marie-Ange's face. "They say that in France?"

Marie-Ange shrugs one shoulder, a demi-gesture that Leah files away with the one-sided smile.

"Moving. Right. Along." The words metal in her mouth. "I love that."

Marie-Ange makes rapid searching movements about her pockets and hair, then pulls sunglasses from her purse, a purse Leah urgently wants to rifle—for passport, license, postcards bearing American addresses. She wants to read the label on Marie-Ange's shirt, the size printed inside her sandals.

"Moving right along." Singsong, this time. "It is definitely what we say, yes."

She sees Marie-Ange close her eyes behind the sunglasses. Perhaps she is gathering herself. Perhaps she is waiting for the blow. Her lids are round, like a doll's, and through the green glass Leah sees a break in the eyeliner where her hand must have trembled that morning. The plump girl is trying, she thinks. Every morning she puts on her eyeliner and sweetly tries. Leah wants to shake her hard and kiss her on the mouth, in that order.

She tries for a note of mild amusement. "So where are you from?"

"Rouen," says Marie-Ange. The eyelids flutter. Fix your

eyeliner, Leah wants to tell her. Put something shiny on your lips. Make me feel the way Terrence feels.

"New Jersey? Really?" says Leah.

"Don't be a bitch," says Marie-Ange. Holding her ground, too—she pronounces it *beach*.

Terrence appears to be taking inventory of the breasts. No. He is probably studying brushstrokes. He has saved for this trip for three years; he has seven days; breasts he can see at home.

Marie-Ange softens the accent. "The Louvre," she says, "has a room of Delacroix you will not believe. Let us go, yes?"

"First tell me," says Leah. They are both watching Terrence, who is now in the next gallery and has started to glance around.

"Fuck you," says Marie-Ange mildly.

"Fuck you too," says Leah, and feels every hair follicle on her body stiffen.

Marie-Ange slants her a long green look through the sunglasses. Then she takes one finger and licks the tip of it. Then she runs it down the gooseflesh on Leah's arm, leaving behind a narrow streak of cold.

"Okay," she says, as if that had settled something. "Chicago."

It's the first time Leah's deliberately been a *beach*. She likes it, likes how her entire body feels like a fist tightening around something stolen.

"Thank you," she says in two musical notes, like a doorbell.

Thinking: you are mine; you belong to me.

Marie-Ange steps closer to Leah, as if to share some murmured observation. Plea for secrecy, thinks Leah—which she will grant. The secret a sticky bond between them, leading to glances over coffee cups and awkward half-smiles, Terrence unsuspecting.

"You want to know something?" says Marie-Ange, sounding, incredibly, still French. "You suck at museums. You suck at chess. Maybe you suck at being his girlfriend, I don't know. So what? Do I give you *sheet*?"

And how is it possible that Leah's stolen the prize, yet Marie-Ange has won? Because Leah cannot slap; she can't call out *Terrence, listen to this*. She sucks at museums and she sucks at being a girlfriend. A siren goes off in her head, crying in discordant syllables like a Parisian ambulance; it freezes all traffic in her cerebral cortex. When she finally thinks of a thing to say, the moment dissipates. Marie-Ange lapses back into communion with Atala.

"Ex*cuse* me?" says Leah, to no one in particular.

Terrence drifts back in their direction, ready to move right along. Marie-Ange stands with chin raised, the sunglasses odd but dramatic. Brave, Leah thinks. Girl invents herself. Sticks to her story. Brave.

Plus she has no intention of being alone in the Louvre with Terrence; she requires Marie-Ange's presence at this moment as much as Marie-Ange presumably requires her silence.

Did he tell her Leah was his girlfriend?

She tries to sound darkly ironic, though mostly it just sounds like trying. "Lead on," she says, addressing Marie-Ange's back. "We say that too."

⬿

The Delacroix room has fat, croaking floorboards, and it is to the asynchronous music of footfalls that Leah falls in love.

His face is lit against a velvet-black ground, as if the painter had raised a candle in the dark. It's a broad face, the bones a temple to the golden mean. The mouth is wide, the stare sensual. It is a stare of waiting sheets, full of the bed, and it is a bed Leah believes she could slip into without fear.

Eugène Delacroix wears a wine-red sweater. The tips of his white collar, incandescent, jut out above.

She steps closer, mindful of the guard on his folding chair who may even now be gauging her proximity to the canvas. Delacroix fixes his eyes on her. His irises are obsidian. He gazes straight into the crenellations of her brain.

Anonyme, the label reads, about 1820.

The gates of the walled city that is Leah Levinson slide open on their oiled tracks.

Oh.

She feels the breadth of Delacroix's neck as if her hand lay on his flesh. She feels his presence around her like a cape unfurled. He awaits her response. She feels this too.

Yes, she says. It is still not a word she is used to saying.

Three feet from the guard, who sits with his elbows on his knees, she stands without motion or muscle and allows Eugène Delacroix to love her. First he kisses her mouth. He smells of turpentine and musk. He grabs sheafs of her hair in his two broad hands. His voice is tobacco and dry leaves; he has not spoken to a woman since 1863 but he is speaking now, he is being cryptic and she cannot understand. He bites her lower lip and says: Your body is harboring an ancient knowledge. He draws her hands up under his sweater and says: You have only to let it go.

She feels physically stunned, as if she had stepped off a curb and into the path of a bus.

I don't get it, she says.

She stares at Delacroix while Terrence and Marie-Ange traverse the room of his work, work that Leah does not wish to see. Instead she memorizes his hairline, his leonine cheekbones, while Delacroix smolders with his obsidian hunger. She's just getting started on the bridge of his nose when Terrence touches her elbow.

Leah doesn't move.

From her physio book she recalls a rabbit who was forced to look at a pattern of black stripes. They killed him then, developed his retinas, printed them like film. Watery but unmistakeable, there were the bars—the rabbit's last vision, wavering on paper in hazy grays.

Behind her, she feels Marie-Ange lean lightly into Terrence, the bodily equivalent of *hey*. Hears her say, *sotto voce*: "Your girlfriend, she have the Stendhal syndrome."

Leah wants the face of Delacroix to be the last true thing she ever sees.

At the Café Cador she presses Terrence to face the window, though it means he will sit by Marie-Ange. She wants him to have *un balcon*, the little present of a view, to make up for gifts not given. The green marble tabletop is scribbled with cracks, but Leah won't study its geology till a waiter swipes it clean: it is braceleted with water, blessed with crumbs. She looks away.

Two tables over, a woman gestures passionately with her upper body. Her thin shoulders swoop and drop. Her head bobs and ducks.

"Try not to stare," says Terrence gently.

Impossible. The silver chignon. The way she davens like a bird.

"I think she's beautiful."

"You're kidding," says Terrence.

Marie-Ange appears riveted by their slight discord. Leah tries to ignore her; she suspects Marie-Ange can read her retinas. "I mean it," she tells Terrence. "I mean she used to be beautiful. I bet when she was twenty she had boyfriends all over the place. Her husband seems to adore her."

"Indulge me," says Terrence. "Please don't stare."

Marie-Ange finally twists around to see.

"I'm just watching the husband," says Leah, but obediently she starts studying the menu.

In a soft voice Terrence says, "It embarrasses me." Which hardly seems fair now that she's just quit rubber-necking, and now Rebuked Leah wants to crawl under the table, she hears him thinking *You're only in Paris because I brought you, because I paid.*

"But she is right," says Marie-Ange. "Look at the husband. It is sweet." The accent recalibrated—this time an American girl too long in Paris, grown confused about her vowels.

Terrence closes his guide to the Louvre and pretends to look around for a waiter. When he is finished not-looking he says: "What's sweet?"

Marie-Ange says, "He act like she is normal."

Leah nods, though her mind is on another, more embedded kind of beauty: the neurons themselves, spidery of axon, tendrilled of dendrite, misfiring to a symphony that no one hears. She imagines the woman's brain to be an orchestra hall with empty seats of carmine velvet. The floor is swept, the conductor long gone home to his wife, and yet one violinist stays on, perversely, playing violent sonatas in a key for which no music was ever written. Leah finds this more moving than flying buttresses, more profound than the verdegris saints who step down the roof of Notre Dame. But it is beyond her power to explain.

"He love her very much, I think," says Marie-Ange.

Leah looks up, amazed. She wonders if Marie-Ange is not her rival after all. She thinks perhaps Marie-Ange is the angel of Chicago, France, flung down to their table to teach Leah this: That she does not pay the proper attentions, not to guidebooks, not to Paris, not to love.

"I think he trained himself not to see," says Terrence, and this time he really is signaling for a waiter, one hand in the air.

Marie-Ange plants her hands at the edge of her chair and leans forward, deepening her bosom into a major architectural feature. Entablature, thinks Leah. Frieze. Her mother would know.

"Look at you two," says Marie-Ange. "You look like you just crawled out of the catacombs. You are supposed to be having fun in Paris. I propose—"

But I don't *want* to have fun in Paris, Leah thinks, what is wrong with me, I don't want to have fun, I want to be abandoned by Terrence, I want my face to go slack with sorrow, I want to die like Atala for love of Delacroix—

"I propose," says Marie-Ange, "to show you a true French meal."

Leah tells Terrence at the hotel, when they are getting ready for dinner.

He looks up from clipping his toenails. "Well," he says, and laughs. "It was kind of obvious." Carefully, he deposits a paring into the cup of his hand. His arches are high, the feet almost balletic except for a loopy signature of hair across the toes.

"You knew? How did you know?"

"She told me. While you were swooning over that Delacroix painting. But I could tell." He opens his hand over the wastebacket. "She's just living out some fantasy," he says. "It wasn't personal."

He peels off his t-shirt, and under cover of argument Leah inspects his chest. It is opaline, like the chests of the Christs.

"It wasn't *personal?*"

Terrence shrugs. "She was playing around. She knows a lot about art. Aren't you getting ready?"

"I am ready." She changes into a top she had washed in the sink; it's stiff in places, damp in others. "I can't believe you *knew*," she says. "What's her real name?"

"Maryann," says Terrence. "She doesn't like it."

She watches him pull on a clean shirt, white like all his other shirts. "This is a silly conversation," he says. "She spends all day showing us the Louvre. She's taking us to a bistro we'd never find on our own." *Because you haven't read the guidebook.* "Why are you so angry?"

"She lied," says Leah, as if that is the worst thing a person could do.

"Well," he says in a reasonable voice, and stops.

She waits for him to admit the obvious: they were, in fact, suckered. She was suckered by the accent and the caramel skin and he was suckered by the art-history tour and the damn balconies. He only agreed to dinner so Marie-Ange wouldn't writhe in embarrassment for the rest of her life. He'll put an end to it after dessert; he'll say they need some time alone. Then he'll take Leah to the catacombs. In fact he is becoming drawn to her; he wants them to start over, and he is willing to be patient. Tonight they will move clumsily toward each other beneath the white matelassé spread, murmuring in fake French accents and cracking up, and being patient together. Maybe even a bit less patient than the night before.

"Well," he says again. "Were you lying about doing the reading? Were you lying about planning the Louvre? Were you—" He pounds a fist into the wardrobe door. Then he looks hard at the ceiling. A thin crack meanders above the bed, directing tributaries toward the windows. "I'm not angry about those things," he says. And then: "Maybe a little. Maybe I am."

Leah feels the imprint of a palm on her face, as hot and swift as if she has been struck. She presses her fingers to her throat, where there seems to be a hole.

"You've been pretending too," says Terrence. "About a lot of stuff, if you ask me."

The hole in her throat gets hot. It swells to the size of a coal. A jagged noise comes out of it. She cannot look at him.

Terrence drops his voice into a gentler register. "Don't punish yourself," he says quietly. "You didn't do anything bad. We just care about different things. I'm going to dinner. You should come."

The bed has long since stopped pulsing. It is just a place to curl up, after Terrence leaves, so she can biopsy her inner self for rotten spots—all the horrible *beach* parts that need cutting out.

"I bet she knows the perfect little place," says Leah. "Oh, God. I'm sorry. I didn't say that. I didn't mean it."

Terrence tugs on a clean sock.

"Please could we forget I said that?"

She is growing desperate. She has bumped something fragile off a shelf, a thing she must snatch from the air before it shatters. And she is genuinely surprised to realize that she is going to just stand there and let it fall.

"Are you going to sleep with her?"

Terrence puts his owlish glasses back on. He looks nice. He probably smells nice. He has sensual feet, crucifixion feet. His irises appear to be cut from sheetmetal. He no longer reminds her of wheat.

He might be safe to go to bed with now.

"Wouldn't you be happier," he says, reaching for his windbreaker, "if I did?"

She opens the casement window and sits on the bed, tapping her cigarette into a little white dish and staring into the dark.

So French, her mother would say, to hang treillage on an air-shaft wall. No light for vines, but look, Leah, what beauty a person can make—like sketching a garden in the air.

When the cigarette is finished she gets up and swallows two Prontalgines. Rinses the toothbrush glass and fills it with Medoc. Drinks one glass, changes into her night-gown, turns out the lamp. Drinks another. Falls and falls through a bottomless airshaft until she lands on something soft.

Honking of pigeon, hiss of traffic: he's phoning from the street. Is it morning? The airshaft has faded to pale gray. His half of the bed is still neat. *Oh God.*

"Oh, God," Leah says into the phone.

"Are you okay?"

"I feel awful." She means her body, the way her eyeballs are packed with lava and the top of her head is screwed on too tight, but then she remembers that she feels awful in other ways, deserved ways, so that for once she has said exactly the right thing.

"Don't feel awful," he says. "Come have breakfast."

Leah takes a deep breath and lets it out slowly. "Okay," she says. This morning, she will try to act with grace. She will move very slowly and order the intravenous coffee and she will try to act with grace. Fifteen minutes, he tells her: Café Atelier. She steps into the tub, drops the French shower. It whips around, spraying two walls and the ceiling. She makes it in seventeen minutes without mopping up.

Her *café crème* waits on the table in a ten-sided cup, covered with a saucer: forgiveness. Two paper tubes of sugar lie empty in the ashtray.

"Hi," he says.

His shirt is wrinkled. Also he smells of Marie-Ange. Specifically he smells of her toothpaste—Leah can see it, an exhausted tube on a graceful, ancient porcelain sink that's gone yellow in spots, like ivory. And he's cut himself shaving, though the blood is dry. She could have told him: if it's in the shower, it's probably dull. Women can shave with goddamn butter knives, she could have said.

She empties the cup in one long and grateful pull. "More," she says. "Please more." It's early but the waiters are dressed in black. She stretches her neck to the left and hears a sound like crumpling paper. Is a person's neck supposed to crumple? A woman marches toward them with a relentless tap of heels and a dachshund on a leash.

"Okay," says Terrence. "What do you want to do?"

The woman slides into a banquette, tugs the dachshund under the table, and places one navy slingback decisively on the leash.

All Leah knows is that he ordered her coffee. All she knows is he is here. In deference to that one fact she struggles not to light up. She figures she has about thirty seconds before she caves.

"I messed up your trip." She wants to say *ruined* but it's too painful; there is no hope for *ruined*. "I'm really sorry."

The dachshund sits twitching at the woman's feet, beseeching her stockinged calves.

"I'm thinking I should pay you back," she says. "For everything."

Terrence hesitates. Leah can hardly bear to watch his face. It looks like wheat again. Instead she watches the little dog, ears like ponytails, as it turns twice, plants its front paws on the woman's knees, and looks up with prayer in its eyes.

She is tired of being afraid. She feels sure that Delacroix could advise her, in some elliptical way.

"I invited you," says Terrence. He reaches across the little table and takes her hand. It is the first time, really, that he has touched her in such a small and specific way. His fingers are warm. Leah accepts this gift of his hand. Maybe all she is supposed to do is like him. Or simply see him. See him and like him just a little. It doesn't have to be so complicated, she thinks.

Lap. The dachshund wants lap. Even Leah can tell this, and she is not overly fond of dogs. When they invent a self-cleaning dog, she likes to say, maybe then. But this one looks washed; it has shiny hair. *Lap.*

"I thought I could do it," says Leah. "When I said yes."

"Rethink it."

Leah looks up, startled. She likes it, likes how the wheat has stopped rustling, how the air has gone perfectly still.

"I can't really pay you back. I can barely afford the roach bombs."

"I know," says Terrence. "Put my hand on your breast."

At the next table the woman looks briefly at the dog, then away. Her back is straight, her heart is closed, her hands are on the table.

"*Excuse* me?"

Virginity is a state of mind. Leah has read that sentence about a hundred times. If it were true she would only have read it once. She thinks about Philip, who rocked himself to sleep, who wanted to see if he could speak that language men and women speak. Some nights Philip twisted through the Ramble seeking men without names. There were mornings, she was sure, that his leather jacket smelled of the bark of Chinese elms, the knees of his jeans redolent with crushed grass.

"I'm serious. Put my hand on your breast."

Terrence wants the language. He wants every word. He wants to smell the moment on her skin. It is no more than he would want from any woman. It is no more than he deserves.

She pulls his palm toward her. She holds it there until her body makes slight alterations. Then she flushes deeply and lets it go and lights a cigarette, jetting the smoke high over his head.

"Maybe you could show me—maybe there are things—." The dachshund circles twice and curls up in defeat. "Or you could stay with Marie-Ange," she says. "If you want."

He reaches across the table and takes her cigarette. He stubs it in the ashtray, not quite finishing the job.

"I don't want," he says.

The waiter brings another *café crème* and a slip of white paper, which she picks up. Out on Boulevard Montparnasse, cars suddenly start parking down the exact middle of the street.

"No," says Terrence. "You get the next. Let's go back to the hotel."

She is out of Prontalgine. She is out of time. She takes one sip and pretends to let the coffee cool.

"Can I ask you a question about Marie-Ange?"

"Not about last night."

But Leah has no desire to ask about last night. She is strangely grateful for the breach.

"What's that thing she said I had?"

"Drink some water," says Terrence. "You don't drink enough water. What thing?"

"Some syndrome," says Leah.

"Fantastic," he says. He rakes his hair with excited fingers. His irises look like gold. "Stendhal syndrome. I bet it's here." He pulls a paperback from his windbreaker pocket: *Responses to Art*. Terrence was right. They care about different things. Thirty-seven bridges, all of them crossing the Seine.

He scans the index, riffles backward through the pages. "The first time Stendhal saw Florence," he says, "he almost lost his mind. Here. Listen to this."

I was in a sort of ecstacy.

She watches his eyes track. He seems to be skimming for choice phrases. *Absorbed in the contemplation of sublime beauty . . . I reached the point where one encounters celestial sensations. Everything spoke so vividly to my soul.*

"That's lovely," says Leah. "Contemplation of sublime beauty." She tries to focus on the words, not on looking like a person who remembers her Stendhal.

"He was literally driven half mad by art," says Terrence. "They say it happens." He closes his eyes for a moment. "No one in my family has ever been to Europe," he says. "My parents have never seen the ocean. And here I am. Listen." *I had palpitations of the heart. I walked with the fear of falling.*

Leah stares at him. All her life she has walked with the fear of falling.

Terrence closes the book. "Come on," he says. He pushes his chair back, then hesitates. "I thought Paris might do that to me," he says. "I'm still sane, though. What about you?"

Her body is harboring an ancient knowledge.

It is time to let go.

The catacomb stairs, a ribbony twist of stone, drill into the earth. Her feet nuzzle for balance at each step like blind fish. Sixty. Seventy. Walls barely further apart than her own shoulders—she could get stuck.

Ninety. A hundred. Footsteps pounding far below. It's a tight spiral; she can't see up or down. Hundred-twenty. Can't panic because can't reverse. Reverse would force the stream to flow backward, up the helix.

Hundred-forty. Hundred-fifty. She loses count. Bad thing, to lose count. Whispers *oh God oh God* in time to her own footfalls.

At last the cochlear staircase deposits her in a small bunker, where two tourists are examining photographs on the walls. The pictures show bones and skulls assembled, like beads or shells, into implausibly decorative arrangements. Leah grapples with the captions. Latin roots prick at her memory: *ossements, mortels, innocents.*

She is deep under Paris, in a concrete crypt with a man in a blue sportcoat and his girl, who swings a Kodak Instamatic by the strap.

She is deep under Paris in a pool of dim light with two strangers who will not help her if the fear hits.

She is deep under Paris with two utter uncaring strangers, and it is a good thing someone has a camera because they are standing at the very threshhold of the empire of death. They all know this because it says so, chiseled into a lintel:

Arrête! C'est ici l'empire de la mort.

It persuaded the Nazis, Leah reads; they never went deeper, or they would have found the Resistance radios.

The blue man is tall and wide of shoulder: Leah finds this reassuring. She lets the couple go first, then steps after them into a tunnel. It was a goddamn mine, wasn't it, before they started dragging in their dead. She knows what a mine is—shafts and black burrows, with collapsible pockets of air. If she gets any more scared she might grab the man's hand, she might turn up her face and whisper, *s'il vous plait?* His girlfriend will stand respectfully back, and he will say what Leah already knows; he will weave his fingers through her hair and tell her: *Je m'appelle Eugène.*

She follows the blue man through passages so long she loses count again and so low at times they both duck. She swings on ropes of darkness between the gray lights. Ahead of her the blue man lopes and stoops, and she focuses on his jacket and prays.

In her prayer, he has long, supple wings. Their tips drag on the ground as he turns around.

Stop fighting, he says, gazing with goodness and mercy at the exact center of her forehead. Let it go.

And then the tunnel widens into a corridor, and the empire of death turns out to be insanely beautiful, after all.

Bones encrust the corridor walls. Femurs, she guesses by their length, stacked like ornamental brickwork, knobby ends out. Packed tight, the bone-walls rise to nearly her height.

Enchanted, she edges forward. Bones beyond counting. Contents of an overpacked *cimetière*: they dug it up, hauled the skeletons here. Now it's all passageways embroidered with bone, the tunnels looping and intersecting, most of them gated off, unlit—and also forbidden: on this Fodor's is explicit. She waits.

After a few minutes, the tourists turn a corner.

Alone, she examines the bones up close. They've been dipped into sugar: granular, where she expected smooth. A few have snapped; they look like sea sponge inside. She puts her hand in her pocket. Keep from touching.

Keep from *stealing*, because what Leah really wants is one of the skulls with which the bone walls are studded. Clearly others have plucked a few of the skulls, leaving empty chalices of air.

The girlfriend laughs. The blue man blinks back into view, vanishes around another corner.

Leah feels her ribcage opening to the tomb. She feels the clocks of her cells tick to midnight, and stop. Before a cross of skulls, she resists the urge to kneel. Instead she listens, and hears water dripping. It must be coursing through the rock. No—knifing through it, she is sure. Fracturing the catacombs, undetectable by any instrument save her own fear.

As she walks, listening to the mine approach collapse, her socks grow wet in her Keds. Up ahead, around untold corners, she hears the girlfriend's voice nattering in the empire of death: "Where do you want to pose at?"

"Pose? Oh, my God," the blue man says. "Bones upon bones. Wait."

It's dry where he's stopped. He's aiming a flashlight. Leah, catching up, sees words she cannot fully parse chiseled into the wall.

Ainsi tout passe sur la terre
Esprit, beauté, graces, talent
Telle est un fleur éphémère
Que renverse le moindre vent.

"Thus everything passes through the earth," says the man. He speaks English with a German accent. Language of her grandmother's enemy. "Mind, beauty, grace, talent," he says. "Like an ephemeral flower that is—" He sucks air between his teeth. "That is knocked over in the slightest wind."

"Perfect," says the girl. "Don't move." An ice-blue flash: Leah closes her eyes.

Thus everything passes through the earth—yes. The water is nothing; it is just a thin stream. Emboldened, she rubs a loose femur with a thumb. Sniffs it. Touches her tongue to the rough span. It smells faintly of old books, triggers salt receptors on her tongue. Like a pebble from a distant shore, it tastes of an ocean she has not yet seen.

Acknowledgments

I am deeply, happily indebted to Joy Harris, Jim Krusoe, and Rob Spillman.

May I also thank Gabriel Fried, poet and surgeon—the perfect editor. And for reading, guidance and other sustenance, I am so grateful to Natalie Baszile, Pia Ehrhardt, Judith Freeman, Jan Gottlieb, Heather Hartley, Tara Ison, Bern Landis, Erica Landis, Lou Mathews, Susan Moorhead, Maxine Nunes, Mary Otis, Rachel Resnick, Claire Whitcomb, and the members of Jim Krusoe's amazing creative writing workshop at Santa Monica College.

Finally, my gratitude to everyone at Persea Books, particularly Karen Braziller, Michael Braziller, Leslie Goldman, and Rita Lascaro, and to the members of Gabriel Fried's publishing practicum at the University of Missouri—especially Tressa Canaday, Emily Coleman, Mollie Esposito and Thomas Kane—for their ardent and arduous work on production and publicity.